"Why *is Famine Ghost* outstanding? Even extraordinary? It tells the story of the Famine in a vibrant, colorful way. It includes well-developed fictional characters and, at times, even humor. The book is illustrated with drawings from contemporary newspapers and other sources. Most are from *The Illustrated London News*. This news magazine was hostile to the Irish. However, even those who worked for it felt sorry for the suffering in Ireland. This is shown in sympathetic pictures."

"It is remarkable that the author can bring this utterly grim event to colorful life. O'Keefe makes the story come alive by using a vigorous and memorable story line. He develops the story with fictional characters but constantly with The Great Famine as the background."

Frank West, "Irish Books and Plays in Review."

Irish American News. October 2011

"*Famine Ghost* is a book of historical fiction, the story of the Irish Famine (1845-1850) as seen through the eyes of young Johnjoe Kevane. He and his family are evicted from their cottage in Dingle. Disdaining the option of life in the local workhouse, the Kevanes sail in a coffin ship to Grosse Ile in Canada. Johnjoe keeps a diary of his family's suffering in the dark bowels of the overcrowded ship. When his parents die of ship fever-typhus-Johnjoe returns home to exact revenge on the landlord, Major Mahon."

"O'Keefe has delicately balanced history with touching humanity and humor. He has provided readers with a vivid tale, surprising in all the right ways, and an unabashed glimpse into the shocking truth of the Irish Famine. A masterful read cover to cover."

Sara Wolski, literary agent

"Famine Ghost captures the realities of the 1845-1850 Great Irish Famine and is filled with valuable research on the tragedy. An imaginative and thoughtful author, O'Keefe has a real gift for the dialog and pace of language of 19th century Ireland. His vivid portrayal and historical perspective bring the hardships of Ireland's troubles to our awareness in the 21st century, like no other book."

--Helen Gallagher, *Computer Clarity*, www.cclarity.com

Acknowledgements

I would like to thank my wife Phyllis for her patience,
Jim Kozicki for his reading, Alan Gbur for his computer
help, and Frank West for his encouragement.

SURVIVORS OF THE IRISH GREAT HUNGER, 1845–1850

Jack O'Keefe, PhD

iUniverse LLC
Bloomington

SURVIVORS OF THE IRISH GREAT HUNGER, 1845–1850

iUniverse books may be ordered through booksellers or by contacting:

iUniverse
1663 Liberty Drive
Bloomington, IN 47403
www.iuniverse.com
1-800-Authors (1-800-288-4677)

Because of the dynamic nature of the Internet, any web addresses or links contained in this book may have changed since publication and may no longer be valid. The views expressed in this work are solely those of the author and do not necessarily reflect the views of the publisher, and the publisher hereby disclaims any responsibility for them.

Any people depicted in stock imagery provided by Thinkstock are models, and such images are being used for illustrative purposes only.

Certain stock imagery © Thinkstock.

ISBN: 978-1-4759-9581-7 (sc)
ISBN: 978-1-4759-9582-4 (e)

Library of Congress Control Number: 2013913010

Printed in the United States of America.

iUniverse rev. date: 9/9/2013

On Sunday October 24, 1999, Gaelic Park dedicated a memorial to the millions of Irish men, women and children who either died of starvation, or who were forced to emigrate during the dark days of the Irish Potato Famine of 1845 – 1850. The sculpture, commissioned and paid for by Gaelic Park, is located next to the main building in a place of remembrance. Headstones in the background denote the one million in Ireland who perished of famine or hunger-related diseases. Designed by Fr. Anthony Brankin, a pastor at St. Odilo Church in Berwyn near Chicago, the memorial is filled with Irish symbols, such as the Celtic cross, the farmer's cottage, the coffin ship, the Irish harp, and the rosary in the father's right hand.

Thanks to Father Brankin, Gaelic Park, and to Brother Tom Collins who took the photograph.

PREFACE

Why write a book about The Great Hunger? My son Denis found my first book <u>Famine Ghost</u> depressing because it describes the horrors inflicted on the Irish in the Famine and he's right. Academics too find the Great Hunger difficult to assimilate: "Readers of the published and unpublished materials on the Great Famine, the dominant feeling evoked is one of sadness—sadness for all that horror and all that suffering and sadness about the failures at all levels to stop that suffering." *Atlas of the Great Irish Famine* Introduction (xvi). The authors of the *Atlas* state that "their study seeks to understand the Irish Famine and its consequences. It is an act of commemoration of the known and unknown dead of the Famine and of the millions who had to flee Ireland." (xvi).

Perhaps one example will be representative of the pain the Irish endured in thousands of cottages throughout the land. An American widow and philanthropist, Asenath Nicholson, describes one such hovel: "A cabin was seen one day a little out of the town, when a man had the curiosity to open it, and in a corner he found a family of the father, mother and two children, lying in close compact. The father was considerably decomposed; the mother, it appeared, had died last and probably fastened the door, which was the custom when all hope was extinguished, to get into the darkest corner and die where passers-by could not see them. Such family scenes were quite common, and the cabin was generally pulled down over them as a grave." *Lights and Shades of Ireland* quoted by Lorraine Chadwick in *Atlas of the Great Irish Famine* (480).

How "common" were such scenes? John Mitchel, Irish patriot and writer, lived during the Famine and was imprisoned for fourteen years for treason against England later but escaped from Tasmania. He renders this account:

> "How an island which is said to be an integral part of the richest empire in the globe and the most fertile part of that empire—should in five years lose two and a half millions of its people (more than one fourth) by hunger and fever the consequences of hunger, and flight beyond the sea to escape from hunger. . . ."
>
> "There began (in 1847) to be an eager desire in England to get rid of the Celts by emigration; for though they were perishing fast by hunger and typhus, they were not perishing fast enough."
>
> John Mitchel. Quoted in *The Irish Famine* (190).

Mother England wished to hide the hunger and deaths in Ireland: "At the height of the crisis, P.M. John Russell in the Commons refused to provide an estimate of famine deaths." Quoted in *Atlas* (170). Cormac O'Grada asserts "that the lower the death toll, the less the blame. And if mortality were higher it was argued that no mid-nineteenth-century government could have alleviated such a problem over a lengthy period." Quoted in *Atlas*, Introduction (xiv).

It is no wonder that Russell refused to give an estimate of Famine dead. According to O'Grada in the *Atlas*, "The best scholarly consensus is that about one million died of famine-related diseases between 1846 and 1851 . . . Europe's greatest natural disaster of the nineteenth century. . . . (170).

Survivors of the Great Hunger tells the story of the Kavanagh family who lived through the Famine and its aftermath. James Palmerston, son of Lord John Palmerston twice prime minister of England, represents the cruelty of Britain toward Ireland. *Survivors of the Great Hunger* ends on a hopeful note—the generosity of today's Irish for the suffering of famine-afflicted nations of the Third World. As Tim Pat Coogan writes in *The Famine Plot*, "it is not unreasonable to hope that a country that could weather the trauma [of the Famine] can also emerge from its current difficulties. A land that could survive the Famine can survive almost any thing. "(235).

John Waters in "Confronting the Ghosts Our Past" explains "there is pain in Irish society that is not being admitted. It is there in the shapes of our society, in our congenital inability to realize our potential. . . . surveys inform us that Irish people don't want to hear about the Famine. Two life times, our grandparents—yours and mine were adults in the Famine period. We don't have to look too far to find its primary sources." "Confronting the Ghosts of Our Past." Quoted in Hayden *Irish Hunger* (28-29). Waters also writes we need "a new dream. . . . but before that dream must come the memory of that nightmare that we have never allowed ourselves to recall." (31).

In an interview with the <u>Chicago Tribune</u>, Holocaust writer Elie Wiesel responds to people urging him to turn away from writing about the barbarities of the concentration camps by saying "Memory has its own mystery and its own mysterious power. Without memory there is no culture. . . . We Jews especially, are defined by our memory and by our link to memory, our passion for memory. Even though our history is painful, my job as a teacher, as a witness, is to give hope." (November 12, 2012).

Wiesel has a point. The Irish Great Hunger is part of the country's collective memory, and we Irish and Irish-Americans should know about it.

THE ACT OF UNION

To comprehend The Great Hunger, we must first understand the Act of Union (1801, 1802), which forced Ireland to become part of the United Kingdom.

One of the negotiators for the dissolution of the Irish Parliament was Britain's Lord Lieutenant for Ireland Lord Cornwallis who asserted "I am working with the most corrupt people under heaven [English landlords]. . . . I despise myself every hour for engaging in such work." "Cornwallis, *enwikipedia The Free Encyclopedia.*

Why did England demand the Act of Union? Because Ireland was Britain's breadbasket. Cecil Woodham-Smith, an authority on the Irish Famine, wrote in <u>The Great Hunger</u> that no issue has provoked so much anger and embittered relations between England and Ireland as "the indisputable fact that huge quantities of food were exported from Ireland to England throughout the period when the people of Ireland were dying of starvation. Ireland remained a net exporter of food throughout most of the five-year famine." nd.state.

Landowners, civil servants, the ruling classes, the bankers, and the "royals" benefited the most from Irish exports. Many of them were absentee landlords sucking money from their Irish estates while living in England or France. As Joel Mokyr explains, "The real problem was that Ireland was considered by Britain as an alien and even hostile country." Quoted by William J. Smyth, *Atlas* (56).

Tim Pat Coogan in "'The Lessons of the Famine for Today" names names: "But is was the Act of Union which took away the Irish Parliament and created the situation whereby when the Famine struck, its handling was entrusted to a handful of British servants, chiefly the head of the Treasury, Sir Charles Trevelyan." Quoted in Hayden (166).

The archives of the British Museum provide damning statistics about the amount of food snatched from Ireland. Cormac O'Grada explains that Britain exported 3,251,907 bushels of corn and 257,257 sheep in 1845 and 480,827 swine and 186,483 cows in 1846. nd.state.

Historian Christine Kinealy in nd.state documents that England imported 9,992 calves and 4,000 horses and ponies and 1,336,200 pigs from Ireland during 1846-1850. The English imported 1,336,200 gallons of grain-derived alcohol and 822,681 gallons of butter to England during the first nine months of "Black '47."

One central fact explains the evils of The Great Hunger: Ireland did not govern itself, England did. Peter Gray asserts that "The cause of culpable neglect of the consequences of policies leading to mass starvation is indisputable." Quoted by Smyth, *Atlas* (53).

In *This Great Calamity*, Kinealy explains "Ireland may have been a part of the United Kingdom, but its place within it was hardly that of an equal partner or even that of a young sibling;: in the words of Ttevelyan Ireland was a 'prodigal son' who had to be forcibly brought under parental control. If, as some people stated, the Famine was a punishment from God, the punitive relief measures did nothing to diminish this belief." (357).

1779 Samuel Johnson counseled an Irishman, "Do not unite wish us. We should unite with you only to rob you." Lord Byron called the Act of Union "a union of a shark with its prey." And it wasn't as if the British government was unaware of the disaster in Ireland. Lord Clarendon, Lord Lieutenant of Ireland, wrote to Prime Minister Lord John Russell about the House of Commons: "I don't think there is another legislature in Europe that would disregard such suffering as now exists in the west of Ireland, or coldly persist in a policy of extermination." In 1849 the British head of the Poor Law commission, Edward Twistleton, resigned because "many were wasting away in the west of Ireland and that it is quite possible to prevent the death of any from starvation by the advance of a few hundred pounds." Twistleton quit his post because "the destitution here is so horrible, and the indifference of the House of Commons to it so manifest, that I am an unfit agent of a policy that must be one of extermination." "Twistleton," *en.wikipedia. The Free Encyclopedia.*

Peter Gray explains the social background of the Famine: "In Britain The Great Irish Famine occurred in an existing ideological context that had already pathologized the backwardness of Ireland and prescribed a reconstructive regime. Ireland differed from other famine-stricken European countries in being interpreted through the lens of colonialism. . . .

What made the Irish experience unique in terms of state response was the British perception of the potato failure as an opportunity rather than an obstacle, an opportunity to deny the benefits of common nationality until Irish society had been remodeled according to British norms." Quoted in *Atlas* (485).

Opposed to providing relief for Ireland were important Englishmen. Nassau Senior, a political economist at Oxford and an advisor to the government, saw The Great Hunger as a partial solution to the Irish problem: "the famine in Ireland would not kill more than a million people and that would be scarcely [hardly] enough to do any good." Quoted in Thomas Gallagher, *Paddy's Lament* (85). Lord Tennyson, Poet Laureate, had another solution: "Could not anyone blow up that horrible island with dynamite and carry it off in pieces—a long way off?" Quoted in Thomas Gallagher, *Paddy's Lament* (89). This after England forced the Irish to join the Act of Union.

The Village of Killard in Kilrush Union, County Clare.

Illustrated London News - 1849

Deserted Village

English Bully

As they were cleaning up thistles from the sheep meadow near their cottage in Listowel, Sean Kavanagh with the outdoor look of a farmer and his small son heard a man on horseback pounding towards them. Sweeping his nine-year-old son Joseph into his arms, Sean covered him with his body, but the brown horse drove right at them, its hooves cutting his shoulders and clipping Joseph in the head, knocking him unconscious. The burly rider hurled a leather bag of coins at the father saying. "Here's for the brat. "After taking one look at his bleeding son, Sean ran over to the horseman, Palmerston, yanked him from his horse, and grabbed the coins. Palmerston's companion Dorset hung back and watched.

"What are you doing," Palmerston roared.

"Going to get help for my son. You better pray he's all right, or else I'll beat you bloody."

After Sean reached St. Michael's along Listowel Road, a ride of ten minutes, Joseph was conscious and mumbling. He brought his son to Sister Clare, a Mercy nun who was nurse, cook, and teacher in the orphanage and school. She had been a nurse in Dublin. She was instructing eight girls in the knitting room. She shrieked at all the blood pouring from Joseph's wound: "What happened?" she asked Kavanagh.

"Palmerston rode us down in our field," Sean answered.

"The brute," she said. Regaining her composure, Sister Clare told Sean, "Get me a bucket of water from the kitchen with some towels and soap for cleaning the wound. Then put the kettle on for some hot water."

As Sister Clare began to clean the wound, Joseph started to speak, "Me head hurts. Did that man run us down?"

"Yes," his father said, "but I'm going for the sheriff."

"Hush, now, Joseph," said Sister Clare giving him a cup of hot buttered rum. "Get this in you. Sip it slowly. You'll feel better." The wound on

Joseph's head extended the length of his forehead just below the line of his red hair and the red freckles popping over his face. Once the drink began to take effect, Sister Clare closed the cut with narrow thread. A farmer's daughter, Sister Clare had joined the Mercy nuns and worked as a nurse in Dublin hospitals. She told Sean that Joseph would stay overnight until the stitches took hold.

Sean rode Palmerston's horse and raced to tell his wife Mary what had happened. "Mary, Palmerston ran down Joseph and me with his horse and knocked him unconscious. Sister Clare is sewing the wound right now, but he's alert and coming round."

"Jesus, Mary, and Joseph. The man ran you down?" Mary was a beauty with raven hair and a temper.

"Yes, then he threw some coins at me as if he could buy his way out of trouble."

Mary said, "Go fetch Nellie and Josie to watch these babies, and I'll ride back with you to St. Michael's to see Joseph."

Sean got Josie and Nellie to watch the children. As the couple rode on Palmerston's horse, Sean said "Mary, there's more. I yanked Palmerston from his horse and told him I would beat him senseless."

"I don't blame you. If you didn't I would have, but see Father Malloy and ask his advice."

Father Malloy had been pastor of St. Michael's orphanage since Sean had lived there when his parents died twenty years before. The priest had a ruddy face and a shock of white hair. After hearing Sean's story, he said, "Go see Sheriff Costello right now or else he'll have only Palmerston's tale."

When Sean arrived at Sheriff Costello's office in Listowel, a frame building in the center of town, he found Palmerston there ahead of him, having been given a ride by Dorset, the latter his friend. Stomping around, Palmerston bellowed: "Here's the brigand who knocked me down, threatened my life, and stole my horse. Arrest him."

"Have you told the sheriff you rode down me and my little Joseph?" Sean asked.

"Some urchin. Why should I care about him?"

"He's my son. "Do you have children, Mr. Palmerston?" Sean asked.

"No."

"I thought not. You're too callous. I took your horse to rush my son to St. Michael's to have Sister Clare sew up his wound," Sean said.

A kind, just man, Sheriff Costello had a round friendly face. He tried to settle things down: "Mr. Palmerston, did you deliberately ride over this man and his child?"

"I was hunting, and they were in my way."

"Sheriff, my son will wear a scar on his face forever. He's resting right now at St. Michael's," Sean said. "We're hoping he'll be fine tomorrow."

"Thank God," said the sheriff.

"I want Kavanagh arrested immediately," Palmerston insisted.

Sean said, "I want to file charges against Mr. Palmerston for assault. He even threw a few coins at my feet trying to buy his way out of trouble." Sean pitched the coins back at Palmerston., and they clattered on the sheriff's floor.

Sheriff Costello said, "Mr. Palmerston, you've done a great wrong here. I'll not arrest Mr. Kavanagh. Instead I'll try to dissuade him from charging you for your attack"

"Costello, I'll have your job for this. And, Kavanagh, I'll make you pay," shouted Palmerston as he stomped from of the sheriff's office.

Once Palmerston had gone, Costello spoke to Sean, "You'll have to walk softly around that blackguard. He's cut from the same cloth as the evil landlord Gray."

"He also threatened you, Sheriff," said Sean.

"I'm not worried. I'm well in with the people, and Palmerston has already made a bad name for himself."

"Sheriff, I can't prove anything, but this accident may have been deliberate. Last week I turned down his offer to manage his farm and estate. This may be his retaliation," said Sean.

"Sean, let's keep this to ourselves. Meanwhile try to stay out of harm's way. I hope your son will recover soon."

"Thanks."

When Sean reached St. Michael's, Joseph was resting peacefully, Mary and Sister Clare by his side. He reported to them and to Father Malloy what the sheriff had decided. Dorset had given Palmerston a ride to pick up his horse at the school, the landlord still in a rage.

"You bloody Papists, some day we'll be rid of you all," Palmerston yelled. "And my father is a member of Cabinet. At this very moment, my father is planning to attack the American Union. We've already built and sent three ships to the Confederacy. Once we attend to the North, we'll come back here to clean out all you Catholic vermin."

"You English have done your worst, Palmerston, and we're still here," Father Malloy retorted. "If you have no better success in the Civil War, you will give up that too. And mind what happened to your predecessor lying dead in the barnyard mud."

"Is that a threat, Malloy?"

"It's history, Palmerston."

PALMERSTON'S OFFER

The week before, James Palmerston, a local landlord, had summoned Sean Kavanagh to visit him at his estate. When Palmerston and Dorset had first arrived at the estate from England, they found it in shambles. Bushes and thistles had grown unchecked, making the land unsuitable for farming and for grazing sheep and cows, which would need cultivated corn for feeding. Palmerston hired ten laborers from town to make the place livable. After several weeks of cleaning and painting, he realized he would need a competent farmer to supervise additional workers and later to evict tenants. Palmerston went to Mayor Kelly or of Listowel and asked, "Who is the most competent farmer in the area?"

The mayor replied, "Sean Kavanagh. He attended the Quaker model farm in Colmanstown, Galway, where he learned to grow a diversity of crops—corn, flax, turnips, cabbage, oats, and wheat." Sean Kavanagh, owned a small farm close by, which he had bought from a previous landlord, so wanting to see firsthand Kavanagh's work, Palmerston and Dorset rode to survey it. They found a variety of crops, a small pen for pigs, a dozen sheep, and a few cows. The good reports were true: Kavanagh was his man.

Father Malloy had tipped Sean off that Palmerston might want to hire him to manage his estate, a task Sean couldn't and wouldn't take the job on. Making his way up the gravel driveway, Sean used the brass knocker on the white door. A servant girl, pretty but harried, wearing a starched white dress answered.

"I'm here to see Mr. Palmerston," Sean said

" Is he expecting you, Sir?" the girl asked.

"Yes, Sean Kavanagh is my name."

She offered Sean a seat on a bench in a long hallway.

After a few minutes, a handsome, thickset man in his forties limped toward Sean using a cane. A permanent sneer marred his good looks. "It took you long enough to get here," Palmerston grumbled. He didn't offer to shake Sean's hand and left him standing in the hall. Palmerston said, "I'll come straight to the point. I want you to manage my farm and to collect my rents. I'll provide you and your family with a cottage on the property and a share of the profits."

"Sir, that's a generous offer, but I cannot accept. I have my own farm and five children to raise. I would, however, be happy to assist at planting and harvest times."

"You realize, Kavanagh, that I could make trouble for you."

"But I've given you no cause, Sir."

"Not doing what I want is cause enough."

When Sean returned home, his wife Mary and he discussed Palmerston's offer: "Sean, you can't take over the man's farm. You're overworked and not home enough as it is."

"You're right, Mary. Also working for him would put me under his thumb, and he wants to make me his gombeen man [rent collector for the landlord] terrorizing and driving off tenants—which I never would do, the same evil that the dragoons did to my own family in Ballyristeen years ago."

"Sure, go and see Father Malloy. At the same time, you can bring Sister Clare some milk for the children at St Michael's." Sister Clare was the Mercy nun in charge of the orphans at St. Michael's.

When Sean met Sister Clare and Father Malloy, he told them of his interview with Palmerston, the priest told him, "He's another land-grabbber just like Gray driving tenants from their land and making them poor. Avoid him as much as you can." Father Malloy was a priest of late middle age with a shock of white hair. He had been founder and pastor of St.Michael's for twenty-five years.

THE ELDER PALMERSTON

Born in 1784, Lord John Palmerston was twice Prime Minister of England. Father of James, Palmerston was an aristocratic lecher. Nicknamed "Lord Cupid" for his affairs with Lady Jersey, Princes Dorothy de Lievin, and Lady Cowper, he was avaricious. To make more money from pastureland in Ireland by raising sheep, he evicted 1000 poor tenants from their farms on his land during the worst of The Great Hunger (An Gorta Mor) in 1847. His agents packed these poor people on eleven "coffin ships" to Grosse Ile in Canada. Because of the crowded conditions aboard ship, many emigrants succumbed to typhus, known as ship fever, and were buried at sea or in mass graves at Grosse Ile. Norita Fleming, a modern scholar, asserts, "it is commonly accepted that from Ireland to Grosse Ile, in the ocean graveyard, bodies could form a continuous chain of burial crosses." O'Keefe, *Famine Ghost* (11).

Adam Ferric, a member of the Legislative Council of Canada, wrote to the English Parliament protesting the treatment of the passengers aboard the Lord Ashburton, the last ship Palmerston had sent: Those who survived the crossing "arrived almost in a state of nudity. The food on board was of the worst description. The captain permitted no exercise aboard ship. The mortality rate was upwards of 25 percent, and there were no food, clothes, nor the two pounds and five pounds Palmerston's agents had promised them on arrival." Woodham-Smith, *The Great Hunger* (223).

Ferric's letter caused a stir in Parliament, but Palmerston denied the charges and blamed his agents. Because of his prestige and power, Parliament soon forgot the accusations. ("Emigration: Departure, Crossing and Arrival, in Ireland " *Great Irish Famine* Unit V).

Young Palmerston

For all his high status, Lord John Palmerston couldn't avert tragedy in his own family when his eldest son James was born with a clubfoot, the left leg turned at a right angle, which made this leg shorter than the other forcing him to use a cane to walk. To the dismay of his father, riding, racing, and hunting, the Lord's favorite pastimes, were impossible for the young boy. Later he learned to ride with a cane strapped to his saddle, but dismounting was very difficult and he fell often.

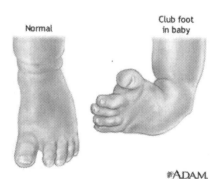

(Club foot and Metatarsus adductus. metatarsus adductus clubfoot)

To compensate for his disability, James became aggressive and domineering, especially with girls and young women, a trait he had acquired from his father. He forced himself on the serving girls at Hampshire, and they avoided him whenever they could. Despite being punished by his father for his behavior, he was incorrigible. At boarding school James was excellent in his studies, but his disability made him easy prey for the taunts of his classmates, so he struck back against them.

In school Palmerston met another boy with a clubfoot, a "new boy," Jeremy Dorset, whom he determined to help. During meals some boys badgered Jeremy, calling him "cripple" and "gimp" and denying him a seat at table. Clomping over to the boys, Palmerston grabbed the worst offender by his neck and threw him against the table, scattering food all over. "Jeremy, sit here," Palmerston roared, giving his quaking friend the bully's seat. When the master of the dining hall walked into the room and surveyed the damage, he asked, "Who is responsible for this chaos?"

No one spoke up except for Jeremy Dorset who said "Those boys refused to give me a seat at table until James forced them. He did it for me. I'll clean up, Sir."

"No. Palmerston, you must put this place right or suffer face ten lashes," the master said.

"The lashes, Sir. These reprobates brought on the damage."

James had made one friend among his peers, tutoring Dorset in his studies and also teaching him to ride and to dismount from his horse with the help of a cane. In his turn Dorset exercised a calming influence on this tutor, showing him that his disability need not make him strike out against the world.

Vexed by his oldest son and anxious to get him out of his sight, Lord Palmerston decided to lease him land near Listowel, Ireland, to manage—the Cowper Estate—part of 12,000 acres given to the family by Cromwell when he pillaged Ireland in 1649 and the 1650s.

As for Dorset, his mother loved him, but his father and brothers treated him as a pariah. Because of his disability, he was no good at games or, later, at farming. He had to use a cane and lurched from side to side when he walked. His father was happy to see his son attend boarding school where he wouldn't have to watch the boy's daily struggles. With James Palmerston's help, Jeremy became good at his studies, but he faced a bleak future like clerking in a business, which was boring and paid little. When his friend Palmerston offered him a position to help him run the estate in Ireland where he could indulge his pastime of riding, he jumped at the chance.

Before he left for his estate, James received this advice from his father: "Follow the same policy I used. Clear off as poor many tenants as possible. Find a local who will extort the rent for you, and then have the dragoons burn and tumble their cottages. Ignorant papists. Convert the land to pasture. You'll earn far more money than collecting rent from small farmers."

SEAN KAVANAGH'S LIFE

Listowel Famine Cemetery

Every Sunday after Mass, Sean and Mary Kavanagh with her two sisters, Josie and Nellie Mullins, visited the "Famine Graveyard" in Listowel where their parents lay after their deaths from typhus. The Kavanagh children, four girls and a boy, accompanied them. Families of The Great Hunger victims had neglected the cemetery either because of their own illness leaving them too weak to care for the plots or simply because of the inroads of time. Overgrown bushes, brambles and thistles with their thorny weeds covered the ground. The passage of the years and the heaving of the ground had caused broken and cracked headstones, like an old man's mouth full of rotten and missing teeth. The Kavanaghs had kept the Mullins' plot cleared and neat. Sean had had a white headstone erected with the inscription "Michael and Delia Mullins Died of the fever in the Year of Our Lord 1547." This year, also known as Black '47, the worst year of the Famine. The family put two blankets on the ground to kneel on for saying the rosary.

Mary had told the children much of the story of her life, that Sean and Brother Leonard, a Christian Brother, had cared for her father in his death throes after their mother had died, and then brought them to St. Michael's where Father Malloy and Sister Clare, a Mercy nun, on loan to Father Malloy from the Mother General of the Mercy order. Sister Clare supervised the orphanage and served as cook, knitting teacher, and counselor. She had raised the Mullins' girls and dozens of others.

This Sunday showed off blue skies with skylarks soaring high above them with their sweet song and finches flashing gold in the rosebush Sean had planted.

Rosemary, at eleven, the oldest Kavanagh child, said "Da, we've learned much of Mam's family. What about yours?"

For a moment Sean looked stricken but recovered quickly: "Rosemary, you're right. Their story, really my story, is so painful that it's hard for me to tell. But I owe it to my parents and to you that you learn about your grandparents."

His wife Mary interjected, "Sean, you don't have to do this if the memories hurt so much." She held his hand and kissed him.

"Thanks, my love, but the children should learn of their grandparents."

The family grew hushed as they sensed the emotions bubbling up inside their father. **My parents, Sean and Delia Kavanagh raised me on a small farm near Dingle. The land was beautiful, Conor Pass and the Brandon Mountains to the north, Dingle Bay at our doorstep.**

We were poor but happy, feeding ourselves on a plot of potatoes and the odd salmon. We paid rent to the landlord until the potato blight struck in 1845 and destroyed our food. The dragoons burned and tore down our cottage in 1847 when we could no longer pay rent. All we could do was watch the destruction.

The bailiff ordered us to the workhouse, but one look was enough. The place was infested with fever, people living on top of one another. My Da decided we should make the long walk to Dublin, just over 200 miles. It took us five days. Often we got a ride from a kind farmer.

The girls began to cry about what their Da and grandparents had suffered, but Sean reassured them. "I survived and am here now to tell you about it. I'm coming to the hardest part of the story now, and we're close to the end."

Evicted *by Lady Butler, 1890, University College, Dublin*

Evicted constitutes a new direction in Irish rural art. Portraying the after-effects of the destruction of the peasant woman's cabin, the beauty of the landscape (the Wicklow hills) complements the plight of the inhabitants. She too is a victim of historic exploitation, with no rights over the land she inhabits.

THE DEPARTURE.

The Departure

STEVE TAYLOR VIEWS OF THE FAMINE

"There are usually a large number of spectators at the dock-gates to witness the final departure of the noble ship, with its large freight of human beings. . . As the ship is towed out, hats are raised, handkerchiefs are waved, and a loud and long-continued shout of farewell is raised from the shore, and cordially responded to from the ship. It is then, if at any time, that the eyes of the emigrants begin to moisten with regret at the thought that they are looking for the last time at the old country-- that country which, although, in all probability, associated principally with the remembrance of sorrow and suffering, of semi-starvation, and a constant battle for the merest crust necessary to support existence is, consecrated to their hearts by many a token."

Taylor, *Views of the Famine*

At Dublin Harbor we boarded the ship *Ajax* bound for Canada. There were 110 of us. The voyage lasted two months. We slept in the hold below deck, so tightly crammed together we could sleep only sideways. Because of this people spread typhus to teach other, the lice invading the eyes and ears and any bruises. Many of the passengers died at sea, and the crew slid their bodies into the ocean graveyard. When we arrived at Grosse Ile, the quarantine station for Canada, my Da and Ma died of the fever and sailors buried them there. Though they didn't want me near them for fear of infecting me, I kissed them both and held their hands till the last.

SCENE BETWEEN DECKS

Between Decks

STEVE TAYLOR VIEWS OF THE FAMINE

Rosemary began to cry again, her tears spreading to the little ones. She ran up to her father and hugged him, "Oh, Da, I love you," she said.

"But it ended well," Sean said. "Doctor Douglas and Father Moylan were kind to me there and got me passage on a timber ship sailing to Tralee. I was blessed to meet and marry your mother. The rest you know."

Mary said, "Da suffered more than he's telling you. He's a good, good man."

Rosemary, I lost my parents, but now I have your mother and you children to love."

Josie, Nellie, Mary and all the children gathered around their father to hug and kiss him. Sean didn't tell his children that he had returned to Ireland to shoot and kill the landlord Major Mahon, who had evicted them. Also he didn't tell about his struggle of almost two years on the run from the dragoons, until out of mercy Lieutenant Thomas finally declared him dead of drowning in Galway Bay outside the Claddagh. He had done a great service to Kavanagh by reporting him dead and freeing him from the dragoons.

Sean Kavanagh did not tell his children he was the assassin in this newspaper account:

"Ejectment Murder—As Major Mahon, a gentleman holding large estates in Roscommon was returning home to continue the conacre system about twenty minutes past six o'clock on the evening of Monday, from a meeting of the board of guardians of the Roscommon union, he was shot dead by an assassin, about four miles from Strokestown. . . . The victim exclaimed, "Oh, God" and spoke no more. Major Mahon was formerly in the 95th Dragoons, now Lancers, and succeeded in the inheritance of the late Lord Harland's estates about two years ago, the rental being about 10,000 pounds. The people were said to be displeased with him for two reasons. The first was his refusal to continue the conacre system [the tenants divided the land among themselves, not the landlord], the second was his clearing away what he deemed the surplus population. He chartered two vessels to Canada and freighted them with his evicted peasantry." (*The Nation*, Dublin, 6 November, 1847).

DISASTER

Before The Great Hunger, Irishmen were eating an average of twelve to fourteen pounds of potatoes a day (*chacha.com.*). The blight, actually a form airborne fungus, phytophthora infestans, probably originated in the Toluca Valley of Mexico and lay in the holds of ships bringing cargo to Ireland. It spread through the country from west to east destroying the staple food of the people. It spread on the leaves of healthy potato plants and destroyed them. For five years the blight ruined the potatoes, the worst year being "Black '47" when the entire crop failed. A French scientist discovered a treatment for the disease—copper sulphate—in 1882.

Healthy potato plant   Diseased potato plant   Blighted potato
"Phytophthora infestans" - en.wikipedia.org/wiki/Phytophthora_infestans)

The potato blight struck Ireland in 1845 destroying the staple food of the people. At first England did nothing to alleviate the suffering of Ireland even though by The Act of Union in 1801, the two were one country, but finally Prime Minister Peel imported 100,000 £ of corn from America which the Irish found difficult to mill for flour--derisively calling the corn "Peel's brimstone." Britain also established public works such as road building for people to earn money.

In 1847 after a change of prime minister to John Russell, England halted the aid, believing the Irish caused their own problems because of their Roman Catholicism. The English government believed in "Providentialism," a free market economy of laissez-faire, by which the English imported tons of corn, barley, and dairy products produced in Ireland while the Irish starved, a million people dead and 21/2 million emigrated.

The British landlords turned the farmland into pastures for grazing sheep and cattle, much more lucrative than collecting rents from poor farmers. Between 1849 and 1854, English landowners evicted nearly 50,000 families. Farmers who had improved their land lost all to evictions. (The History Place-- Irish Potato Famine.).

After the Famine those young men leaving the land caused a scarcity of workers in the country, but instead of hiring young farmers out of work, the landlords used this depopulation to evict more tenants and turned the farmland into larger pastures for grazing. Between 1849 and 1854, the landlords evicted nearly 50,000 families. Farmers who had improved their land lost all to evictions. (The History Place—Irish Potato Famine*)*.

Irish patriot, John Mitchel, said of the Famine: "The English rulers called that famine a dispensation of Providence; and ascribe it entirely to the blight of potatoes. But potatoes failed in like manner all over Europe, yet there was no famine save in Ireland. The British account of the matter is, then, first a fraud, second a blasphemy. The Almighty, indeed, sent the potato blight, but the English created the famine." (The History Place —Irish Potato Famine).

Nightmare

One night when Mary and Sean Kavanagh were sleeping, Sean had a nightmare about his time at Grosse Ile in Canada. "Palmerston, Palmerston," he screamed. Mary woke him up. "Hush, you'll wake the little ones.

When he was awake, he told his wife, "Palmerston, now I recall the name. Doctor Douglas, the chief surgeon at Grosse Ile, told me that Palmerston sent eleven of the worst coffin ships there. His passengers had no food or water when they arrived. No wonder this is a bad man. I'll bet he's a son."

"Sean, you can't do anything about him this hour of the night. Go see Father Malloy at St. Michael's tomorrow and learn what you can. Now go to sleep." But Sean couldn't sleep. Memories of Grosse Ile haunted him.

The next morning Sean recounted his nightmare to Father Malloy. The priest said, "This is Lord John Palmerton's son exiled here because he caused all manner of mischief at his home in Sheffield. His companion Dorset also has a clubfoot, but has a more pleasant demeanor. They both live at the estate, which the father leased to the son. Young Palmerston is a bad actor, that one, and is sure to cause us more trouble."

PALMERSTON AND JOSEPH

With the potato blight over, Sean grew a plot of potatoes behind the house along with oats, barley, and flax. Sean had learned from the Quakers that a variety of crops would protect them from disease, like the fungus that had destroyed the potato crop in 1845-1850. He also raised two milk cows and eight pigs. In addition to the work on his own farm, Sean loaned himself to other farmers to supplement the family income. In their first six years of marriage, Mary had five children underfoot which caused some tension in the house. "Sure, Sean, the only time you're home is to give me more babies. Am I to raise these children all by myself? I'm blessed to have Josie and Nellie, but they'll be leaving soon to marry."

"Mary, we've got to have enough money to build up the farm and raise these babies."

"Yes, but these babies and you are making an old hag out of me."

"Mary, you're as beautiful as the day I married you," Sean said as he circled his arms around her waist.

"That hasn't stopped you from touching and kissing them," Mary said. "And other places too."

"Don't start, Sean. It'll only end in bed."

"That wasn't worrying you last night."

"Don't harp on it, Sean, or else it will mean some cold nights for you."

"Sure, Mary, you know I love you. I'll cut down on hiring myself out and be home more to help you with the little ones."

"Be sure you do."

True to his word, Sean remained home more with Mary and the children. The eldest, Rosemary, was the image of her mother, dark hair. blue eyes, but no freckles. "Thank God, Rosemary doesn't have your freckles," Sean said. "Sure I've been looking at them long enough."

"That hasn't stopped you from touching and kissing them," Mary said. "And other places too."

Their second child was a boy, Joseph, named in honor of the Quaker Joseph Bewley who had helped rescue Sean from Captain Packenham and the dragoons. Unlike his namesake, Joseph was a "divil" into everything as soon as he could crawl. When he was six, Joseph loved to wallow in the pigpen to the exasperation of his mother who scolded him, "You smell like the pigs, Joseph. Maybe you'd like to sleep with them too."

Wise to his mother's teasing, Joseph replied, "Could I, Mam?" Joseph was at his worst when bad weather confined him to their cottage as he pestered his sisters.

Mary said to Sean, "When the weather breaks, you've got to get Joseph outside with you on the farm. I'm tempted to take the strap to him."

"No strap, Mary. There's been enough violence in our country without bringing it home too. Twice Landlord Gray slashed my face with his riding crop before I pitched it into the field."

"Even Sister Clare used to threaten us with her big wooden spoon," Mary replied.

"The only thing Sister Clare ever hit with that spoon was her pots and pans, not even Tommy Linnane who had earned some wallops."

"Which you gave him yourself while telling me to keep my hands off our own," Mary said.

"Yes, because he cut the throats of two of Father Malloy's sheep for the tinkers," Sean said.

THE ENFORCER

English dragoon
"The_Royal_Dragoons" Wikipedia The Free Encyclopedia.

Palmerston was still plotting revenge against Sean Kavanagh. He invited Captain Davison of the Queen's Light Dragoons to his home at the Cowper Estate. Born in Yorkshire, Davison was a career soldier who had served in Gibraltar and in India's Punjab. Tall and spare, the man was devoted to duty. After riding the seventeen miles from his barracks in Tralee, he arrived at Palmerston's house. Palmerston welcomed him into a sitting room stuffed with Queen Anne chairs. The captain received with pleasure a glass of brandy in a cut-glass goblet and a cigar from his host. "This brandy is excellent, Mr. Palmerston."

"Yes, I have it shipped directly from London—genuine armagnac—none of that Irish swill for me."

"May I offer you a cigar, Captain, a Cohiba, directly from Cuba?"

"Yes, thanks. I have not had such pleasures in years, Mr. Palmerston," as his host lit his cigar with a taper.

"You should have some comforts living among these barbarous Papists," Palmerston said. "Roll the cigar around in your mouth so that it burns evenly. Captain, I've asked you here for two reasons. First, I'm soon going to evict some farmers from my land, so that I can turn it into pasture."

"Yes, Mr. Palmerston, for me it's a sad but important duty."

"It's my land, Captain, so I may use it as I wish."

"Yes, Sir."

"Secondly, there is news that some Young Irelanders have escaped from prison in Van Diemen's land."

"Yes, Mr. Palmerston, Thomas Meagher and John Mitchel have fled to America."

"Should have executed them when they had the chance," Palmerton said.

"Yes."

To cause trouble for Sean Kavanagh, Palmerston said, "There's a blackguard who lives near here, Kavanagh, who may well have been involved in the Young Ireland rebellion at Ballingarry some years ago. He was raised in an orphanage, St. Michael's in Listowel."

"Sir, the dragoons arrested a large number of rebels that day. What is the man's full name?" asked Davison.

"Sean Kavanagh."

"Let me check into the matter and see what I can learn."

"Good, report back to me and let me know what you find," Palmerston ordered

When Captain Davison checked the reports of the rebellion at Ballingarry, he could find no mention of Sean Kavanagh. The only reference to Sean Kavanagh was that he had drowned in Galway Bay along with his pursuer, Captain Packenham. Lieutenant Benjamin Thomas, now a captain, had signed the record. An excellent honest soldier, he was again serving in India.

Davison decided he would question the parish priest at St. Michael's about Kavanagh and then interview the man himself. The captain rode the seventeen miles northeast of Listowel to St. Michael's and met Father Malloy, the pastor. A schoolhouse of gray stone stood on one side of the road, a rectory of yellow stucco the other. A meadow filled with sheep flanked the rectory. A priest answered the door and invited Davison in. A turf fire burned in the grate of a fireplace in a small sitting room. "My name is Father Malloy," said the priest.

"I'm Captain Davison from Tralee," the soldier said.

"Is this about Palmerston's running down Joseph Kavanagh, scarring the boy and knocking him unconscious?"

"No, Father, I know nothing about that."

"Well, you should, Captain. With his horse he knocked down the father and his little boy in an open field. Then to assuage his guilt he threw some coins at them, all because Kavanagh refused Palmerston's offer to manage his estate."

"As I say, Father, I know nothing of this."

"Typical landlord behavior towards us Irish. Sheriff Costello has a full report on file about this incident."

"Father, I resent your description of English landlords. They pay my salary and make the country stable"

"Stable in hunger, suffering, and death. Your very presence here deprives Ireland of food."

His face flushed with and anger, Davison asked, "What else do you think of us dragoons?"

"You drive the poor from their homes to go to the workhouse or Canada."

"I'll listen to no more of your invective, Malloy. Where might I find Sean Kavanagh?"

"Two miles east of here on this same road."

Father Malloy was worried about Sean Kavanagh. What could the dragoons want with him?

Davison rode away in a huff, his bright red uniform contrasting with the gray lowering clouds. Everyone on the road ignored him even with his golden sash of captain.

Stopping a farmer with a load of hay on a wagon, Davison asked the man where the Kavanagh house was. "Captain, just off the road. A white farmhouse in good trim."

As Davison approached the farmhouse, he saw a litter of pigs enclosed by a wooden fence. A beautiful woman with raven hair answered his knock. Inside the bright cottage, five children were playing in front of the fire. Paintings of Christ crucified and of his mother Mary hung on the walls. A square wooden table with spindle chairs dominated the kitchen, and a set of stairs led to an upstairs for sleeping. The woman asked, "Are you here to gather more information about Palmerston's attack on our family?"

"No, Mrs. Kavanagh, I wish to speak with your husband."

"He's tending the sheep over the hill with Joseph, the little boy Palmerston tried to maim."

Davison rode up the hill and met a raw-boned man tending a dozen sheep with two border collies and holding the hand of a little boy with an ugly red scar running the width of his forehead.

"Da, is this man going to ride us down too?" the boy asked.

"I hope not," Sean said.

"I'm Captain Davison. Are you Sean Kavanagh?"

"I am. If it's about Palmerston, you can see his handiwork on Joseph's face, a mark he'll wear forever," Sean said.

"No, I wish to speak with you about the revolt at Ballingarry in 1848."

"Sure, I wasn't even near the place. Didn't even hear about it for days after," Sean replied. "I was on my way through the Gap of Dunloe with a Quaker, Joseph Bewley, on our way to Skibbereen with food. Captain Redmond was returning from the battle and was leading a squad of dragoons."

"I know Redmond him well," Davison said, "a good man. He'll verify your story?"

"Yes, if he remembers me. That was ages ago. Mr. Bewley and I pulled to the side of the road and allowed his dragoons to pass."

"He had just come from Skibbereen and warned us. He was right."

"What did you do there?" asked Davison.

"Buried some poor souls in the cemetery of Vicar Townsend, may God rest his soul, and worked in the Quaker soup kitchen. Depressed by the starvation and death in Skibbereen, I went to the Brothers' soup kitchen in Cork run by Brother Leonard and fed starving children," Sean replied.

"All these people will vouch for your presence?"

"Yes, Sean said, "if they can recall that far back."

"Listen, Kavanagh, you appear a decent man. Stay away from Palmerston who has friends in high places."

"I will, Captain. I just hope he leaves me and mine in peace."

On Sean's arrival home, Mary questioned him: "What did the devil want?"

"To see if I was at the revolt of Ballingarry. I'll bet Palmerston put him up to it to harass us," Sean said.

"'Tis no wonder these landlords are in danger the way they carry on."

"Yes, Mary, but I've had my fill of fighting."

" I know, Darling."

Attack on Josie

Josie Mullins lived in a cottage a few yards away built by her brother-in-law Sean Kavanagh. Like her sister Mary, Josie was a beauty, tall, with dark black hair. She had caught the eye of James Palmerston, a local landlord who lusted for her. When she wasn't helping Mary with her five children, she managed a knitting shop in Listowel that sold fine scarves and sweaters. The store the sisters rented was in the middle of the town near the sheriff's office, Sean's idea for safety from thieves and tinkers.

Just as Josie was about to open the shop one morning, a handsome man with a clubfoot and a heavy black thorn stick for a shilllelagh lurched into she shop. "Good morning, Sir. How may I help you?" Josie asked

"My name is Palmerston. Can you knit me a long heavy sweater for me to wear out riding in the damp fields? I have an estate and workers that I must supervise."

"Certainly, Sir. Once I take your measurements and you choose a color." Josie sensed something odd about the man. His face was handsome, but he radiated menace. He clomped around the store and chose a dark green pattern for his sweater.

"I like this," he said. "What does it cost?"

"Three pounds, Sir. It will be ready for you in a week."

During his time in the store, the man made Josie uncomfortable, but she couldn't pinpoint a reason. When two new customers came into the shop, a father and his daughter, Josie was relieved that she would no longer be alone with Palmerston.

Palmerston rode out of town. His plan was to follow Josie home and rape her in a field. After all, no one would believe a peasant girl's word over that of an English gentleman and landlord. He hung back on the road when the girl turned into the field where he had had a fight with Sean Kavanagh. How did this girl know that devil? Josie went into a cottage and

Mary's five young children surrounded her. Palmerston had to postpone fulfilling his lust for another day.

When Josie and Mary talked in the kitchen about Palmerston, Mary asked, "A big walloper of a man with a cane?"

"Yes," Josie answered.

"That's Palmerston, the man who tried to run down Sean and little Joseph. He's a bad man so be careful of him."

Palmerston waited a few days for his chance. On a gray evening he followed Josie from the shop. His companion Dorset was by his side but wanted no part in molesting the girl. Palmerston would have his way with her in a field away from the road before she reached home. He rode up from behind Josie, the soft turf of the ground muffling the sounds of the horse's hoofs. Lunging for her, he grabbed Josie's dress, tearing it. She screamed, "Help! Help!" as he dismounted and said, "I'll have you now, my girl. Don't worry. I leave no woman unsatisfied."

Irish Blackthorn Stick or Shillelagh

Using his cane, Palmerston clambered down from his horse and lumbered after her. Josie picked up the black thorn stick that he had dropped in his haste. It had a heavy knob on top for hitting. Grabbing the cane, she pummeled Palmerston many times about his face and head, blood flowing into his eyes and partially blinding him. He screamed, "You hoor, I'll get you yet." When she was getting away, he clumsily remounted his horse to give chase. At the end of the field hung a low wooden fence to keep cows off the road. Shrubbery covered the fence, and Palmerston drove his horse right into it. The mount broke through, but Palmerston's leg was caught between two wooden bars and snapped as it broke.

Sean Kavanagh heard the screams and ran to the scene. The villain screamed, "Help me. That hussy caused this."

Sean asked Josie, "What's the matter? Why is your dress torn?"

"The devil tried to tear it off me to rape me. He may have broken his leg."

"You," Sean said to Dorset, Palmerston's, companion, "ride to Fr. Malloy's at St. Michael's and have him bring his horse and buggy here. We can transport your master to Dr. Driscoll's in Listowel."

By this time Mary, Josie's sister Mary had joined them and deduced what had happened, "He tried to rape you, didn't he?"

Still in shock, Josie replied, "Yes, so I hit him with his black thorn stick and ran from him. He crashed into the fence chasing me."

Mary put her arm around Josie and led her to their cottage for a cup of tea and some comfort. She gave Josie one of her dresses to replace the one Palmerston had torn.

Lying on the rough ground among pieces of fence, brambles, and thistles, Palmerston screamed, "Help me. She's a dirty hoor. Took her dress off to tempt me."

"You're a liar, Palmerston," Mary said, and ran over to kick him in his good leg.

Sean said, "Now we can add attempted rape to your other crimes."

Sean returned with Father Malloy and a young man from the orphanage. The three men heaved the big man into the priest's horse and trap, Dorset the companion of Palmerston, trailing after them. Palmerston was screaming the whole time, "You fools, go slow. My leg hurts with every bump."

"Keep your mouth shut, you rapist," said Father Malloy, "or we'll dump you out in the middle of the road."

"Where are you taking me?" Palmerston asked.

"To Doctor Driscoll in Listowel," Father Malloy said, "better than you deserve."

When they reached Doctor Driscoll's surgery in Listowel, Palmerston said to him, "Can't you give me anything for the pain? What kind of doctor are you?"

"A good doctor. Unless you wish to transfer to the hospital in Tralee, an hour's journey with your leg," Doctor Driscoll replied.

"What will you do here? " Palmerston asked.

"Put a plaster cast on your leg and a splint to immobilize it. You'll need six weeks of bed rest until the fracture heals," said the doctor. "Meanwhile I'll stitch up the cuts on your head and face."

"Go ahead then," Palmerston growled.

After leaving the doctor, Sean Kavanagh went straight to see Sheriff Costello to report on the attempted rape by Palmerston.

"Good God, Sean. The man is a devil. How did it happen?" the sheriff asked.

"He followed Josie home from the knitting shop where he had ordered a sweater a few days ago. In a sheep field near our cottage, he tore her dress, but Josie grabbed his black thorn stick and hit him about his face and head. He continued to try to chase her down, but she was too fast for him. With his eyes full of blood, he blundered into a cow fence and broke his leg."

"Where is he now?" the sheriff asked.

"At Doctor Driscoll's."

"How is Josie?"

"She has bumps and bruises and is very shaken, but she'll be fine," Sean said.

"Any witnesses?" the sheriff asked.

"His companion Dorset. And there's this," Sean said, handing him the bloody thorn stick. "And her blouse is all torn."

"He's a beast," said the sheriff. "I'll report this to the magistrate who will conduct a hearing. Josie will have to confront him and tell his story."

"She'll do it," Sean said. "As for Palmerston, he'll be recovering at home for six weeks. Just imagine what his housekeeper, Nancy Kelly, must go through."

When Sean arrived home, Mary had helped settle Josie down, putting a blanket around her. Mary said, "Josie will eat with us and spend the night here until the shock wears off."

Sean put his arm around his sister-in-law and said, "Josie, I'm going to train up a border-collie pup which will give you some protection. You did a good job fending off that devil. He's got a broken leg, which will keep him housebound for weeks. I talked to Sheriff Costello who will request a hearing at which you'll have to confront Palmerston."

"Josie began to cry, but said, "I'll do it," she said. "He's evil."

"It might be wise if you don't repair your dress," Sean said. "It will serve as evidence against him."

"But he'll only lie and deny it," Josie said.

Mary replied, "We'll all be there to support you."

"I have an idea that may help us," Sean said. "Bishop Browne of Elphin told me to call on him if there is trouble. This is trouble."

BISHOP BROWNE

Sean made the 170-mile trip to Delphin in Roscommon to see Bishop Browne. The bishop had aged since Sean had seen him six years earlier. "Sean, it's good to see you again in our benighted country. You survived the coffin ships, typhus, and Captain Packenham."

"Bishop, you gave me good advice. As you suggested, I now use the English version of my name "Sean Kavanagh" and barely escaped the clutches of the dragoons in Galway where I fished with the Quakers. I was able to buy a small farm in Listowel and now have five fine children."

Over tea in the bishop's study, Sean unfolded the story of the attack on Josie Mullins to which the priest replied, "Palmerston again, the son of evil Lord Palmerston"

"Bishop, we need a good lawyer to deal with Palmerston in a hearing."

"Sean, I was a barrister myself before I entered the seminary. Though I haven't practiced in years, I still have my lawyer's skills. I'll take on the case myself. Tell Father Malloy that I'll be staying with him while I prepare for the hearing. I'll need the sheriff's reports and then meet with Josie to go over her account."

"She is shy and sweet," Sean said, "but has a good sense of herself; and is not afraid to speak up."

"Good," the bishop said, "they'll try to bully her in court."

THE HEARING

For six weeks until his hearing, Palmerston recuperated at home. Then Doctor Driscoll removed the plaster cast, and in a few days, Palmerston, with Dorset at his side, rode to the town hall in Listowel for the hearing. He had written his father about the charges against him, proclaiming his innocence and asking him to send a lawyer to defend him. Lord Palmerston chose Lionel Herbert, a prominent London defense attorney, and sent him to Listowel for the trial. The magistrate who would pronounce judgment was Thomas Pyncheon, a member of the Anglo-Irish ascendancy from Tralee. Few people knew Pyncheon who would be an unknown quantity at the hearing.

The trial would take place at the town hall, a two-story wooden building that accommodated a hundred people, most of them from Listowel. Josie's family and friends, Doctor Driscoll, Father Malloy and the defendants filled the courthouse.

Magistrate Pyncheon opened proceedings by saying to Bishop Browne, "Bishop, why have you traveled so far from Roscommon to serve in this trial?"

"To assure justice for Josie Mullins, a Catholic, who is not a member of the Protestant ascendancy."

"Do you not think the woman could get a fair trial in our court, Bishop?"

"Mr. Pyncheon, we live under British laws, not Irish ones."

"I assure you, Bishop, that I will conduct a fair hearing," said the magistrate. "Let's begin. Ms. Mullins, please stand and tell us what happened. After you have completed your testimony, Mr. Herbert will question you for the defense and Bishop Browne for your side."

Coached by Bishop Browne to stand tall and erect and to look the magistrate in the eye, Josie began: "I was walking home from our knitting shop in Listowel when I heard a horse coming up behind me into the field near my cottage. The man said, "I'll have you right here. He reached over and tore the top of my dress while he was still mounted."

Palmerston couldn't hold his tongue, interjecting "A dirty lie. The hussy bared her breasts to tempt me."

The magistrate said "Quiet, Mr. Palmerston," and told Josie to continue her account. "As he climbed down from his horse to grab me, he dropped his black thorn stick. I picked it up and used it to fend him off, striking him about his head and face."

Sheriff Costello said, "I would like to introduce the thorn stick as evidence." He gave the magistrate the thorn stick encrusted with dried blood.

Again Palmerston interrupted, "She damn near blinded me. The blood flowed into my eyes, so I couldn't see to guide my horse."

Magistrate Pyncheon was angry, saying "One more outburst, Mr. Palmerston, and you'll be removed from court."

"Ah, Pyncheon, you're nothing but a local. My father in London will put you in your place.once he finishes doing away with the North in the Civil War."

For the first time, Bishop Browne spoke up: "Mr. Pyncheon, this is the second time that the defendant his interrupted the course of this hearing. I move that you find Mr. Palmerston guilty of assault and attempted rape and impose a suitable punishment."

Embarrassed by this turn of events because he knew the bishop was correct, Pyncheon said, "No, we will hear the testimony out and then make our judgment. Mr. Palmerston, you have received your last warning. Ms. Mullins, please continue."

"When I yelled for help, Palmerston climbed back on his horse to pursue me. He crashed into a low wooden fence near the road and injured himself."

"What happened then?" the magistrate asked

"My brother-in-law, Sean Kavanagh, who had heard my screams, came and pulled Palmerston from the bushes with the help of Mr. Dorset. He then rode to St. Michael's to borrow Father Malloy's horse and trap, loaded Palmerston into it, and with Father Malloy drove him to Doctor Driscoll's in Listowel."

"And you, Ms. Mullins, what did you do?" asked Mr. Pyncheon.

"My sister, Mary, took me to her cottage to recover because I was so agitated. She gave me a dress to replace the one Palmerston had torn."

Palmerston's lawyer Herbert spoke for the first time "Ms. Mullins, you mentioned a torn dress. Any proof of that?"

"Yes, Sir," said Josie, "I kept the dress as evidence," taking the green dress from her bag and displaying it to the magistrate. There were two huge rips across the top.

"But Ms. Mullins, you could have made those rips at any time after the alleged attack," said Herbert.

Bishop Browne spoke: "Ms. Mullins is an accomplished knitter and could easily have repaired any damage to the garment."

Herbert asked, "Ms. Mullins, did you ever meet Mr. Palmerston before the incident?"

"Yes, he came into our shop and ordered a long sweater," Josie said.

"At that time did Mr. Palmerston make any advances to you?" asked Herbert.

"No, Sir. Other customers came into the store. I didn't see him again until he assaulted me in the field," said Josie.

The bishop asked Palmerston, "How did you know where to find Ms. Mullins?"

"I saw her on the road before she bared her breasts to tempt me," Palmerston replied.

"Did you follow her into the field?" the bishop asked.

"Yes," Palmerston said

"Why?"

"To find out when my sweater would be ready," Palmerston said.

"But didn't Ms. Mullins tell you the sweater would be ready at the end of that week?" the bishop asked.

"I forget," Palmerston said.

Herbert said, "Ms. Mullins, you've testified that family members came to your aid after the incident. Did anyone else witness your version of events?"

"Yes, Mr. Dorset."

"Is Mr. Dorset present?" the magistrate asked.

A man in a fine gray coat raised his hand and hobbled with his cane from the rear of the hall. Mr. Herbert had coached Dorset about how to reply to any questions.

"Mr. Dorset, what is your position?" asked the magistrate.

"I help manage the estate, Sir."

"With all due respect, Sir, how can you function as a manager with your disability?" the bishop asked.

Reddening, Dorset said, "I mostly ride, but can dismount when necessary."

The magistrate asked "Were you at the scene of the incident?"

"Yes, Sir," Dorset replied.

"What did you see?" Herbert asked.

"I was sitting on my horse at the front of the field near the road," Dorset replied. "I could see Mr. Palmerston and Ms. Mullins exchanging words. Her dress was ripped."

Palmerston and Herbert shared a glance after Dorset's slip-up about the dress. He had departed from the script.

"Was there any attempt by Mr. Palmerston to rape Ms. Mullins?" Herbert asked.

"Not that I could see, Sir," Dorset answered.

Bishop Browne asked, "Did you hear any screams or calls for help from Ms. Mullins?"

"No, Bishop."

"How far away from where you were is the Kavanagh cottage?"

"Less than a quarter mile," Dorset replied.

"How can it be that Ms. Mullins' family heard her scream from inside their cottage and yet you heard nothing?" asked the bishop.

"I don't know," Dorset said.

"Ms. Mullins, Mr. Dorset was at the scene of the incident. What did he do?" asked the bishop.

"Nothing," Josie replied.

"Mr. Dorset, why was Palmerston's mount galloping toward Ms. Mullins if he wasn't trying to chase her?" Bishop Browne asked.

Dorset said, "He must have lost control of his horse."

"But isn't Palmerston an excellent horseman and would it not be strange for him to lose hold of his horse?" the bishop said.

"Yes," Dorset said.

Again Palmerston glanced at Herbert as if to say Dorset had departed again from his prepared answers.

Bishop Browne was pushing Dorset hard: "What exactly is your relationship with the accused?"

"We went to boarding school together in Sheffield, and he asked me to help manage the estate," Dorset said.

"Where do you reside now?" Bishop Browne asked.

"At the Cowper Estate."

"Who pays for your food and lodging?" asked the bishop.

"Mr. Palmerston."

"So, Mr. Dorset, you have a vested interest in the affairs of Mr. Palmerston that might sway your testimony," said Bishop Browne.

Dorset remained silent.

The magistrate spoke, "Mr. Dorset, answer the question. Do you have a vested interest in Mr. Palmerston's innocence."

"I suppose you might say that, Sir," Dorset replied.

Palmerston rolled his eyes in exasperation.

It was time for the lawyers to give their summaries. Mr. Herbert for the defense said, "This is a trial based solely on hearsay. We have only the word of Ms. Mullins as testimony against my client. Mr. Palmerston is a gentleman and a landlord. Ms. Mullins is merely a shopkeeper, a farmer's daughter."

For his part, Bishop Browne said, "Ms. Mullins was the victim of an unprovoked and premeditated assault. Her station in life has nothing to do with guilt or innocence. Palmerston's own words were, 'I'll take you here'. Mr. Palmerston may be many things, but he is not a gentleman. I hope, Mr. Pyncheon, that you find the accused guilty of assault and attempted rape."

Mr. Pyncheon said, "We will now have a fifteen-minute recess until I pronounce judgment."

Palmerston rushed over to Dorset, saying, "You fool, mentioning the torn dress and my riding ability."

"But it was true, " said Dorset.

"If I'm convicted, I'll break your neck," Palmerston threatened.

After the short recess it was time for Magistrate Pyncheon to pronounce judgment "The only witness was Mr. Dorset who saw no attempted rape. I find the defendant not guilty."

The audience in the hall gasped.

"But, Mr. Palmerston, your behavior was at least questionable. You had better reform yourself, no more chasing after young women."

Bishop Browne spoke, "Mr. Pyncheon, you said you would conduct a fair trial. Do you feel this has been fair? The one witness is a friend of the accused, you've seen the ripped dress, and the blood-encrusted cane. You've done a grave injustice to Ms. Mullins. The fact that you had to warn the accused suggests he is guilty, but you English deny us Irish any justice."

"Bishop, but for your clerical station, I would hold you in contempt." Flushed with anger, Pyncheon stormed from the hall.

Bishop Browne and Josie's family rushed up to a console her. Bishop Browne said to her, "You did well and told the truth. You should be proud of yourself. You were a victim of Palmerston and a corrupt English court."

After the trial Jeremy Dorset was sick with himself. Palmerston and Herbert had so cowed him that he had lied and denied seeing the attempted rape of Josie, doing her a grave injustice. The immorality of Palmerston gnawed at his conscience. The man abused Nancy Kelly, the cook and servant girl nightly. When would he stand up for himself? Jeremy had to do something, but what?

Bishop Browne's Warning

When Bishop Browne was making his plans to return to Roscommon, he called Sean Kavanagh aside for a talk: "Sean, beware of the Whiteboys. They cloak themselves all in white and wear masks for fear of the authorities. They harass farmers for paying rent to the landlords and use violence and take a sacred oath. They combat collecting of tithes to the Church of England and evictions—good things, but the Church has outlawed them. Even Daniel O'Connell is against them."

Sean said, "Sheriff Costello told me they destroy fences and maim livestock. They're also known as 'ribbon men' who consider their marauding as retributive justice for the evils the landlords have done. They'll only bring the dragoons down on us."

"Yes," said the Bishop "Another point, the North in the American Civil War is recruiting Irish men for their Civil War. Stay out of it. Many young Irish have joined the Irish Brigade in New York. You've got a family to protect. As I say, stay out of it."

"I will," Sean said. "I'm through with fighting."

Nancy Kelly

Nancy Kelly, a girl of eighteen, was Palmerston's cook, housekeeper, and unwilling bedmate. She was a "cottage girl," the name for an Irish woman whose parents were dead, on her own with no dowry. At first she had been glad to accept the job Palmerston offered. Once a week she went into Listowel for flour, sugar, coffee, and other provisions. Very often as she did her shopping, she would meet Sister Clare who was always friendly. One Monday morning, the two had tea in the back of the shop. When the nun asked "How are you keeping", Nancy let tears make their way down her face.

"What's the matter, Nancy?"

"Sister, you're so good and pure, it's hard for me to tell you this."

Sister Clare noticed the bruising on the girl's face.

"Palmerston has made me his harlot, forcing me to go to bed with him most nights. The Drink makes him randy, and he does terrible things to me."

"Nancy," Sister Clare said, "you can't hold yourself responsible for things over which you have no control. You must eat and live."

"I know, Sister, that's the only thing keeping me there," Nancy said, still crying. "All he cares about is having me. The only good thing about it he's in such a hurry that it doesn't take long. 'My kitchen wench,' he calls me."

"What if we could find you another place?" Sister Clare asked. Patting her hand, the nun said, "I'll inquire around and see if we can find you a decent position."

"Oh, thanks, Sister."

The Tinkers

Irish tinker caravan

"Travelers" or "Tinkers," came from the word for "tinsmiths." The Irish called them "tinkers,"a pejorative term. People scorned them for being nomadic, never settling in one place. Although they were itinerants, like Gypsies, they were genetically pure Irish. They rode in horse-drawn caravans, pitching tents in open fields for cooking and sleeping. They practiced very poor hygiene, their children dirty and disheveled, probably to make them more needy in appearance when going out to beg. Particularly bad were their teeth, most of them toothless by middle age. They made money from their trade of repairing pots and pans cleaning chimneys, fashioning jewelry to sell, making silver and gold trappings for horses and working as itinerants during the harvest. On the road they begged meals from farmers. Girls were betrothed as young as twelve, but only to another tinker. For this reason, many women were unhappy in their marriages and abandoned their families.

Many Irish hated the tinkers, not only for their nomadic way of life but for trampling on crops, polluting wells, and stealing livestock. When they passed through a town, people sprinkled them with holy water and threw rocks at them.

One peculiar superstition of the Irish on St. Patrick's Day was tinkers would overturn rocks and boulder in streams and rivers to drive out the cold of winter. Tinkers went from village to village, and townspeople paid them for this work.

boarderancestry.com

44

One afternoon a band or "Travelers" or "Tinkers," came to St. Michael's to beg for food. Sister Clare was always glad to feed them, and she instructed her students to call them "travelers, not "tinkers," a term they hated. She said, "People scorn them for being nomadic, never settling in one place, usually no more than two weeks."

Father Malloy joined the conversation: "You've seen them on the road in horse-drawn caravans, pitching tents in open fields for cooking and sleeping." Then Sister Clare interjected, "The travelers practice very poor hygiene, not cleaning themselves up well, leading to disease among the children."

JOSIE'S DESPAIR

Josie Mullins had hardly done a mean thing in her life, except for exchanging the odd bit of gossip in the dormitory at St. Michael's. Yet now she was a victim, assaulted by a would-be rapist who emerged scot-free in his trial before an English magistrate. Though two months had passed since the attack, she wondered for days what kind and merciful Jesus would allow this to happen to her? Simmering with revenge against Palmerston, she had no options open to her. Her family and the villagers in Listowel had shown her great sympathy, but it wasn't enough.

Her sister Mary began to notice a change in Josie. Normally talkative, Josie played easily with the children. Now she became quiet and withdrawn and stopped visiting. When Mary mentioned this to Sean, he said "She's still grieving, in mourning over the farce of the Palmerston hearing. Sure, the whole town knows she was innocent. Give her time; she'll come around."

But Sean was also worried about Josie, having also seen the change in her personality. He decided to confide in Sister Clare whom Josie had always loved and relied upon for advice. Sean walked to St. Michael's and found the nun preparing dinner for the orphans, pots and pans all around her. "Sister, a quiet word," he said. "Josie has taken the Palmerston assault and the hearing very badly as if she's in mourning"

"How could she not, Sean? That awful man got away with attempted rape, his only punishment he caused himself by crashing into the fence."

"But, Sister, it's been two months since it started, and she's still in a state, not herself at all."

"I'll visit her in the shop soon, and we can talk privately."

PALMERSTON'S ATTACK

Palmerston and Dorset were riding on Listowel Road one afternoon, and while Dorset had exercised a calming influence on Palmerston—his lust for young women ran unabated. His housekeeper and cook, a girl of eighteen, filled his bed every night, but he grew tired of her and sought fresh prey.

A tall girl with ebony hair was holding the reins of the horses pulling the red caravan. She was a beauty with brown eyes and a full figure for a sixteen-year-old. Even her dirty face and ragged clothes failed to conceal her beauty. She caught Palmerston's eye, and he lusted for her.

Palmerston heard that tinker fathers often sold their daughters for sex. He asked the father, Paddy, sitting next to the girl, "How much for a tumble in the field for that one, pointing to the daughter?"

"For ye both or just one?"

When Dorset shook his head "no," Palmerston said, "Just me"

"A crown," the father said. "Siobhan, do what the man wants."

Palmerston flipped the man a crown. The tinker pitched out a rough red blanket to cover the ground in the field for the coupling. The whole family in the caravan watched the scene in silence.

"You'll be well satisfied, my girl," Palmerston said. He tore the girl's dress as he thrust into her roughly. When Palmerston was finished, the girl grabbed her torn dress and limped back to the caravan.

"Not bad for a tinker girl. Any time you want it again, clean yourself up a bit, and come to see me at the Cowper Estate just down the road and over the hills. The name's Palmerston."

SALLY'S TORTURE

Bridge over River Feale near Listowel
Retrieved from **commons.wikimedia.org/wiki/File:Listowel_bridge.jpg**

Sally O'Connor, Siobhan's mother, had been born a traveler, but never had she seen brutality like Palmerston's. She started a row with her husband: "You sold our lovely Siobhan to that beast for sex, and he hurt her. All our children saw it. What kind of a father are you?"

Paddy beat his wife, blackening both her eyes. When the children heard the argument, they scattered from the caravan into the woods nearby.

Having endured years of life with a drunk, Sally decided to end it all. Like a woman possessed, she ran towards the stone bridge over the River

Feale. Awkwardly, Siobhan chased after her mother, "Mam, come back. The man didn't hurt me bad." The father staggered by Drink followed them. The road ran along the edge of the woods with tall oaks on the east side. The river flowed ten feet high over brown boulders. Sally would drown if she jumped. By this time Siobhan was crying to her mother: "Mam, what will happen to the little ones?"

Sally reached the high point of the bridge and plunged into the water. Struggling to stay afloat with her sodden clothes, Sally went under once. Siobhan was ready to jump in after her when a fisherman, Jim Casey, pulled her mother to shore.

"What's the matter with you, woman? Suicide is a mortal sin."

"On, thank you, Sir," Siobhan told the fisherman.

Coming up behind them, Paddy had sobered up from the shock.

Shaking her fist at her husband, Sally screamed, "No more selling our daughter and no more beatings. Next time there may be no one there to save me, and I'll be gone forever. Would God the man wasn't there."

"Yes, love," Paddy said.

The three walked back to the caravan.

Palmerston was having difficulties from an unlikely source, his companion, Dorset, who said to him, "James, you treated that girl very roughly. She even bled and had to limp back to the caravan."

"I paid for her, didn't I?"

"You didn't pay for making her suffer."

"Listen, Jeremy, the girl enjoyed it. Yes, she may have bled a bit, but she took pleasure from me."

"No, James, you brutalized her."

"What do you care? She's only a tinker. I'll bet she does this often. Tinkers sell girls much younger than her. Jeremy, if you don't like the way I act, you can always sail home to England and see what kind of life you can carve out for yourself there. With me you have food, a home, and a job."

"James, you've always been good to me; but if you continue to carry on like this, I will leave. It's better than watching you assault young girls."

Palmerston listened but gave not a care.

When the tinkers reached St. Michael's, they sent the three little ones to beg for food. In return, twelve-year-old Tom would mend any pots and pans. Sister Clare told the boy to bring a large pot for "stirabout," a mixture of cornmeal and rice. When Tommy returned, he repaired the pots and pans. Still in shock over the brutal treatment of Siobhan, he told Sister Clare about Palmerston's attack.

"Was he a big walloper with a club foot?" asked Sister Clare. "Yes," Tommy said, "his name is Palmerston."

Father Malloy kept a flock of sheep in a meadow near his barn, and Tommy marked the place for future stealing as his father had taught him.. Sean Kavanagh had trained two teenagers from St. Michael's to act as shepherds with the help of two of his border collies. When Sister Clare informed Father Malloy about the presence of tinkers and of Palmerston's assault of Siobhan, the priest said, "The man is an animal." The priest summoned his two shepherds and warned them about sheep stealing by the tinkers: "They've stolen from us before, so keep a close eye out. They'll come again."

When Father Malloy was next in Listowel, he told Sheriff Driscoll, "There are tinkers about. We don't mind feeding them, but we have to be on the lookout for sheep stealing."

"That's a good idea, Father. I'll ride around to the other farmers and inform them too. Sure, they'd steal the eye out of your head. The most vulnerable are the widows who have no one to protect them."

"Fine," said Father Malloy, "I'll mention it at Mass Sunday too."

Walking from her shop to home one late afternoon, Josie met a band of tinkers coming against her on the road, their red wagon driven by a dark-haired girl whose ragged clothes failed to mask her beauty. "Do you know where Palmerston lives?" the girl asked Josie.

"I do," she said, "just over those hills to the north, but don't go near the man. He's evil."

"Don't I know it," the girl replied.

"I'm Josie Mullins. Palmerston tried to rape me in a field near my home. He chased me on his horse, but crashed into a fence breaking his leg."

"Good enough for him," the tinker girl said.

Josie then unfolded the story of the trial to the girl whose name was Siobhan O'Connor. She took Josie by the arm and led her into a field out of earshot of the caravan and told her tale: "My father, may God forgive him, sold me for sex to Palmerston for a crown. The man took me roughly, my whole family watching, even my little sisters."

"Jesus, Mary, and Joseph," Josie said, "and I thought my ordeal was bad."

Siobhan said, "Now I want revenge, not only against Palmerston but also my own father. There was another man there too. All he did was watch."

"Though I avoided your suffering, I feel so angry I want revenge too. We've both been his victims," Josie replied.

"My father wants only money and would sell me to Palmerston again."

Siobhan said, "Let's think of some way to get back at that devil. We'll have to keep our plans secret because my father wants only money. About my feelings he cares not a whit."

"A good idea," Josie said, "I want to make the devil pay."

When Siobhan clambered back aboard the wagon, he father asked her what she had been talking about with the girl

"She showed me where Palmerston's house is," said Siobhan.

"Good," her father said. "We'll know where to find him to steal some sheep."

The next day Sister Clare went to see Josie in her knitting shop. "These knits are wonderful," the nun said. "You have learned your craft well. How are you keeping yourself?"

With no pretense, Josie rushed into the sister's arms, "Oh, Sister, I'm miserable. All I ever think about is getting revenge on Palmerston. I carry the attack and him going free like a stone on my heart."

"That's only natural, Josie. The hearing did you a terrible injustice because you were innocent."

"That's just it, Sister, I can't let it go."

"That too is only natural," said Sister Clare.

"Sister, I met a traveler girl on the road. Palmerston raped her—for money paid to her father. She wants revenge too. She wants the two of us to make a scheme to get our retribution."

"Josie, the tinkers are a breed apart. I'm sorry for the poor girl, but there is nothing you can do for her, especially since the man paid the father. The tinkers will handle their own affairs. But that's not you, Josie. You're a kind, sweet girl who will be looking for a husband soon. Is there any man you're seeing?"

"Frank Collins, the grocer's son, but I can hardly look him in the eye after Palmerston's accusations."

"But you know in your heart you did no such evil, even putting yourself at risk fending the beast off."

"But I still feel guilty."

"Feeling guilty doesn't make you guilty," Sister Clare said. "I don't know a lot about the ways of the world, but I do know that women who are molested feel guilt—even though they did nothing to provoke the attack. This is especially true in our church, which is so concerned with sin and remorse. Take up your life again and bury the wrong done to you, like Jesus before Pontius Pilate."

"That's good advice, Sister. I'll try."

"As for getting revenge, it will only darken your heart. Stay clear of the tinker girl."

"But, Sister, that girl suffered more than I did."

"Yes, Josie, but the tinkers have their own ways of dealing with the world..Walk out with Frank Collins or some other good man and marry, putting all this behind you."

"Sister, I know you love me. I'll work on changing my heart."

Ejection

One Sunday afternoon when Palmerston and Dorset were out riding on the estate, they came across the neat white-washed cottage of Michael Moore, a tenant. With a garden of potatoes behind it, the farm was clean and neat, all shrubbery and trees cleared away. Palmerston told Dorset to ride into town and have the sheriff prepare a notice of eviction. But Dorset objected, "Sean, where will these people go if you drive them off?"

"I don't care."

When Michael Moore stepped out of his cottage, he said, "Mr. Palmerston, how can I help you?"

"I like the cut of your land, Moore. I want it for myself. I'm going to evict you."

'But, Sir, my rent is paid up, and I've dug up trees to clear the land."

"No matter, Moore, I want this land for grazing. You have four days to clear out."

"Sir, I have a wife and three little ones who won't have a home."

"That's your problem, Moore."

Moore went to Sean Kavanagh for advice. They recruited Father Malloy, the three men going to see Sheriff Driscoll. The sheriff told them that Palmerston had prepared an eviction notice and that as sheriff he had to uphold the law.

One Monday morning Sean Kavanagh was bringing extra milk for the orphans at St. Michael's when Sister Clare asked him to sit in the kitchen to have some tea. Sister Clare said, "Sean, I need a favor, a big favor."

"Sister, you know that whatever you ask, I'll do it."

"But this may stir up some bad memories for you."

Sean said, "Ask away, Sister."

THE GREY NUNS

The Grey Nuns
Basilica Notre Dame, Montreal~Feeding the Poor
The painting shows St. Marguerite d'Youville distributing bread
to the poor. She founded the community of the Sisters of Charity
(Grey Nuns) in 1747, and was canonized on December 9, 1990.
Photo Nicoletta Siccone,, "Virtual Tourist."

"Gray nuns (Sisters of Charity of Montreal with garb of grey) cared for the sick, carrying women and children in their arms from ships to ambulances. According to Montreal journalist and historian, Edgar Andrew Collard, 30 of 40 nuns who went to help (at Grosse Ile) became ill, with seven of them dying. Other nuns took over, but once the surviving nuns had convalesced, they returned."

"One of our nuns, Sister Paul, who teaches at Mercy Hospital in Boston, wrote me that her family has lost track of her sister, Bridget Carroll, who came to Grosse Ile in 1847, the same summer as you. She learned from me that you had been at Grosse Ile and then she then placed this ad in the *Boston Pilot*:

'18 December 1849

Of Bridget Carroll, a native of Killacooly, parish of Drumcliff, County Sligo, who was taken into Grosse Ile Hospital, below Quebec in June last, and has not been heard from since. Any information respecting her will be thankfully received by her sister, Sister Paul Carroll, Mercy Hospital, Second Street, Boston, Massachusetts.'

"Sister, I may well have been there at the same time. I used to run buckets of water to the suffering souls in the hospital and the fever sheds, but I don't remember her."

Fever Sheds at Grosse Ile

STEVE TAYLOR VIEWS OF THE FAMINE

"Is there any hope, Sean?"

"I don't know, but I can write to Father Moylan, a kind chaplain there. He may know of a list of names of those admitted there or who died there."

"Well, at least that's something," Sister Clare said.

"Another possibility is for your friend to go up there herself, with some family along, and search the records. Neighboring towns like Kingston and Ontario took in some of the sick from Grosse Ile and may have lists of patients."

"God bless you, Sean."

"Sister, if I could I would go there myself; but with Mary and the children, I can't do it. Also, the memories of my Ma and Da would dog me the whole while."

"Sure, I know, Sean. That's why I was reluctant to ask you."

"No matter, Sister. I'll write a letter today and post it tomorrow."

"God thank you, Sean."

A month later a letter from Canada reached Sean. It could only be about Bridget Carroll. Fearing bad news, Sean brought the letter to Sister Clare unopened, so she would have the news first hand.

Sean walked to St. Michael's where he found Sister Clare in the knitting room. "Sister," he said, "I've received a letter from Canada and decided to bring it to you unread."

"I hope it's good news," she said.

She read it aloud to Sean,

> "Dear Sean,
>
> What a pleasure to hear all is well in your life.
>
> I have good news about Bridget Carroll. She survived an attack of typhus and is now living and working with the Grey Nuns in their orphanage in Quebec. Her address is the Grey Nuns, Orphanage of Mary Immaculate, Quebec, Canada.
>
> God bless you and your family. You were a great help to us at Grosse Ile.
>
> Sincerely,
> Your friend,
> Father Peter Moylan"

The letter brought tears to them both. Sister Clare said, "I'll write Sister Paul right away. I can't thank you enough." She hugged him.

"On another matter, Sister, Josie has begun to come around, accepting her feelings about the Palmerston trial. I don't know what you said to her, but it worked. Our family is so grateful for your love and kindness. You do nothing but good."

"Two blessings in one day, thank the Lord," said Sister Clare.

The one problem still vexing Sean Kavanagh was the imminent eviction of the Moore family. Moore had done everything right, paying his rent on time and clearing the land. Now he faced eviction. Sean couldn't help but think of his own family's tumbling in Ballyristeen some thirteen years ago. The rent collector and the dragoons had sent the family to the workhouse and then to the coffin ship *Ajax* where his Ma and Da died of typhus on Grosse Ile. His lasting image would be the nearly naked bodies of his mother and father hoisted from the hold of the ship by a harpoon like the lance that pierced the body of Christ. The laborers then dumped their bodies into a mass grave on the island.

What could he do to prevent of the eviction of the Moore family? The dragoons would come with the rent collector, the destructives, and, of course, Palmerston. They would set fire to the cottage and then knock down the walls.

To save the Moores, Sean had thought of making a personal appeal to Palmerston, but the attacks on Joseph and Josie had soured their relations further.

Sean spoke to Mary while she was making dinner: "Mary, Palmerston will be evicting the Moores in a few days, and I was wondering what I could do to help them."

"Like what?"

"Go to see Palmerston personally and offer to take over the management of his estate in return for allowing the Moores to stay."

"Jesus, Mary, and Joseph, you're off your head altogether. Deal with the bastard who ran Joseph down and tried to rape my sister. And how would she feel if you were to work for him and become his man throwing our friends off their farms?"

"Right enough, Mary, I'd be making a deal with the devil and that would hurt her."

"Sean, you're a sweet, kind man, but you can't save the world. You've plenty of work right here. I feel bad for the Moores too. What you can do is offer them to stay here with us for a few days."

"Right, love. I want no part of conspiracy that would use violence. I've had my fill of that."

"Remember too that Palmerston has the dragoons behind him. We can only pray that he be gone from us," Mary said.

The Tumbling

IRISH EMIGRANTS LEAVING HOME.—THE PRIEST'S BLESSING.

Irish Emigrants Leaving Home. -- The Priest's Blessing, 1851

Steve Taylor Views of the Famine

". . . I came to a sharp turn in the road, in view of that for which we sought, and of which I send you a sketch, namely, the packing and making ready of, I may say, an entire village-- for there were not more than half-a-dozen houses on the spot, and all their former inmates were preparing to leave. Immediately that my rev. friend was recognised, the people gathered about him in the most affectionate manner. . . . He stood for awhile surrounded by the old and the young, the strong and the infirm, on bended knees, and he turned his moistened eyes towards heaven, and asked the blessing of the Almighty upon the wanderers during their long and weary journey."

Steve Taylor Views of the Famine

"The role of eviction in the creation of the Great Famine is central. . . . 97, 248 heads of households were evicted, a total of 579, 036 people." (Toibin 190).

Charles Edward Trevelyan in charge of famine relief for Ireland pronounced that "The only way to prevent the people from becoming habitually dependent on government is to bring the operation [relief] to a close. The uncertainty about the new crop [of potatoes] only makes it more necessary. Whatever may be done hereafter these things should be stopped now or we run the risk of paralyzing all private enterprise and having this country [Ireland] depend on you for an indefinite number of years.

Pat Stack, "The Hunger Years."

From Tralee Road four scarlet-jacketed soldiers from Her Majesty's Light dragoons rode to the Moore farm east of Listowel. Captain Davison, wearing the yellow slash of ribbon signifying his rank, led his troops to another tumbling, boring for them, but tragic for the Moores.

James Palmerston with Dorset in tow met them at the cottage and pointed at the door of the whitewashed house they would soon destroy. Palmerston ordered,

"Captain, leave not one stone standing on another because some of these farmers would sneak back and throw a bit of canvas and live in the remains. They call it a scalp."

Brian Moore in Scalp.

"The ditch side, the dripping rain, and the cold sleet are the covering of the wretched outcast the moment the cabin is tumbled over him; for who dare give him shelter or protection from 'the pelting of the pitiless storm?' Who has the temerity to afford him the ordinary rites of hospitality, when the warrant has been signed for his extinction?"

Steve Taylor Views of the Famine

Captain Davison nodded assent. With their polished boots the dragoons sat mounted at attention with their muskets held across their chests. The appearance of the dragoons contrasted with the shabbiness of the three villagers, "destructives," the Irish called them. Recruited by the dragoons from town, they would do the dirty work, the burning and tearing down of the cottage. They brought sledgehammers and pickaxes to destroy the home of a neighbor.

(http://tee2i.org/topics/ireland)

The rent collector and middle man between the landlord and the tenants, knocked on the door and said, "Michael Moore, it's time for you to leave. Take your belongings outside. We are carrying out Mr. Palmerston's notice of eviction. He's here with the dragoons, so be quick about it."

Weeping, Betty Moore held the hands of her three little ones. In a blue blanket, her husband carried a teakettle, a frying pan, and a black cauldron for hanging over the fire. A crucifix poked out of one corner of the blanket.

A small crowd gathered around the scene fearing a similar fate themselves and showing support for the Moores.

Sean yelled out, "Captain, is this one of the duties that you dragoons boast of?"

"Kavanagh, you'd best keep quiet," Captain Davison yelled.

Father Malloy pulled Sean aside and said, "There's nothing to be gained by antagonizing these soldiers. You'll only make trouble for yourself and your family. Just focus on the Moores."

One of the destructives carried a firebrand into the house and lit it from burning peat. He then turned to his two fellows and set their firebrands blazing. Hurling their burning torches onto the roof, the destructives set the thatched roof ablaze quickly.

The Moores huddled together in the garden and watched their house burn down—the table they used for meals, the chairs they sat on, and the bed they slept in. The horses of the dragoons trampled down their small plot of early potatoes, which had been their main source of food. After two hours the fire cooled, and the destructives attacked the walls of the house with their hammers cracking any boulders, which could make the foundation for a new house. Soot and smoke covered everyone, darkening even the red coats of the dragoons. Only the charred remains of furniture and a few stray stones marked the place where the house once stood.

Father Malloy walked over to Palmerston who watched until the destruction was over. The priest said, "Well, Palmerston, a job well done, making five people homeless, so you can enrich yourself raising sheep."

"It's my land," Palmerston retorted, "and I'll tumble more houses until all you Papists are gone."

"Very Christian of you, Palmerston. I'm sure the Lord Who sees all things will give you a just reward."

"I'll worry about the next life when I'm finished with this one. Meanwhile I'll continue my work," Palmerston said.

"And fine work it is, starving the poor. I suppose your will try to bring your 'work' to America, meddling in their affairs too. Remember that many Irish revolutionaries are fighting in the Civil War, and we Irish have long memories."

From the beginning to the end of the tumbling, the dragoons sat impassively on their mounts providing a show of force that wasn't needed. They had carried out dozens of evictions; and if Palmerston had his way, they would preside at more. What thoughts they had, they kept to themselves.

Sean Kavanagh helped Michael and. Betty Moore move their few belongings to his own house.

The landlords didn't evict all the Irish. An enterprising 54-year priest, Thomas Hore of Wexford, thirty miles east of Dublin, had spent eleven years in Richmond, Virginia. Hore knew that there was cheap and fertile land in America. In 1850 with poverty and death all around him, he decided to rally his flock to escape from Ireland. In a sermon, Father Hore exhorted his parishioners to sail to America. His enterprise was not without personal danger to himself. Dublin Castle sent David Lynch, Police Constable of The Royal Irish Constabulary, who administered Ireland on behalf of Britain's rulers to secretly gather information regarding the planned pilgrimage. He sent a long, handwritten letter outlining Father Hore's activities. Hore was risking treason, even death.

Collecting money from his flock, Father Hore commissioned three ships, the *Ticonderoga*, the *Loodinah*, and the *Chacsa* for the 5000 miles trip across the Atlantic.

The 1500 passengers first reached New Orleans and then Arkansas, but good land was scarce there. In 1851 Father Hore proceeded to Allamakee County in Iowa where he found what he wanted—rich, cheap farmland. Purchasing 2,157 acres at $1.25 each, he distributed the land to his followers who cleared it and used wood from the surrounding forest to build their homes and a two-story house and a farm for Father Hore where he raised cattle and sheep. That same year he founded the church of St. George.

In 1857 he returned to Ireland, leaving 6000 Catholics in his settlement.

Laxton, *The Famine Ships* (3)

Siobhan and Josie

In town Siobhan went to visit Josie in her knitting shop, woolen sweaters of white and green filling the shelves. Siobhan said, "It's time we got revenge on Palmerston."

"No," Josie said. "I've had a change of heart. Thinking about him has consumed me. Now I've distanced myself from those feelings, and I'm at peace."

Siobhan said, "I want to go and rob him of his sheep."

"Good Lord, you'd never get away with it, with the sheriff and the dragoons behind him," Josie said. "They'd hang you for stealing sheep."

"I don't care," Siobhan said. "I want revenge."

Religious Visitation

Sister Clare was a religious Sister of Mercy, an order founded by Mother Catherine McAuley in 1831. Her group became known as the "walking sisters" because instead of living in a convent as contemplatives praying and meditating, they tended to the poor and uneducated on the streets of Dublin. She and her followers devoted their time to acts of charity, such as visiting the sick and imprisoned, managing hospitals, orphanages, and homes for distressed women.

Their work in Dublin attracted Sister Clare, a farm girl, used to labor. She was a member of the sisters on loan to Father Malloy who begged Catherine McAuley for help in running an orphanage and school in the midst of The Great Hunger. Once Sister Clare entered the order, she never looked back.

According to church law, every so many years the Mother General conducted a visitation of each of her sisters to investigate their work and to judge their following of their religious vows: poverty, chastity, obedience, and perseverance in the order. Catherine McCauley found nothing but excellence and kindness in Sister Clare's apostolate. She tended to the sick and dying, taught the orphans in domestic skills like knitting and cooking, and dispensed sound advice to those who wanted it.

Father Malloy feared that the Mother General might haul her back to Dublin. He begged her to let Sister Clare continue at St. Michael's. "Sister, I would be lost without her. She cooks, instructs, and does all manner of charity for the poor, even feeding the tinkers. Please allow her to remain with us. Sure the children love her."

Chuckling, the Mother General said, "Not to worry, Father. I have no intentions of transferring her. I wish I had more like her."

"Thank God," said Father Malloy. "What a relief to me."

"But I must warn you, Father, that there are reports of a terrible Civil

War in America. We may need her nursing skills in the United States. Until then she's yours. One request, Father, that you allow her a week of leave to visit our colleagues in Dublin and see her family in Wexford. I'll send a novice to replace her for the time."

"Fine, Sister, she deserves a break"

Going over to the school to speak again with Sister Clare, the Mother General said, "Father Malloy can't say enough good things about you. I did ask him for a leave of one week for you to visit our nuns in Dublin and your family. You're doing great work here, and God love you for it. But I told him, as I'm telling you, that your nursing skills would be very useful in the American war."

"Thanks, Mother. You're always kind."

NANCY KELLY

For weeks Sister Clare had sought a new situation for Nancy Kelly, so that she could escape Palmerston's abuse. When the housekeeper and nanny for the mayor of Listowel, passed away, the nun spoke to the family who welcomed her recommendation. Brian Shanley and his wife Beatrice lived in a two-floor home in the town. Nancy would help care for their four small children and tend house. No more would she have to endure Palmerston's cruelty and lust. She never even told him that she was leaving, gathering up her few belongings and walking to Listowel on her own. Her former master had acquired such a bad reputation in town that he could find only one person willing to cook and clean for him—Biddy O'Hearn, an unmarried woman in her fifties who could match Palmerston's meanness.

One Saturday morning as the van of travelers stopped by St. Michael's, O'Connor sent Siobhan out to beg. Carrying an empty pot, Siobhan met Sister Clare in the kitchen. The nun asked, "What is your name, girl?"

"Siobhan O'Connor."

"I'm Sister Clare. This stirabout I'm making is just about ready. It has to cool. We'll have a cup of tea and a chat meanwhile. How many do you have to feed?"

"My parents and me and four little ones."

"We have plenty for you," said the nun. "Now that the famine has let up, are you travelers any better off?"

"Yes, some farmers give us their dying or dead sheep or horse. People call us 'knackers' for eating horse meat." Siobhan greedily drank her tea.

"Another cup?" Sister Clare asked.

"Yes, please."

Impressed by the woman's kindness, Siobhan spilled out her story. "Sometimes my father sells me to men for sex."

"A sad way to earn money," Sister Clare said without any reproach.

"Just a few days ago a man named Palmerston took me brutally." Tears ran down the girl's cheeks in rivulets cutting through the dirt from driving on the road.

Handing her a clean handkerchief, Sister Clare said, "How awful for you."

"But I'm going to get revenge on him."

"How?"

With my father to rob him, even to kill him," Siobhan said.

"But if you're Catholic, that would be a terrible sin and might mean hanging for you."

"Sister, I'll risk it."

As Siobhan got up to go, Sister Clare said, "Wipe your face with the handkerchief to dry your tears and keep it. The stirabout is now cool, so bring it back to your family," Sister Clare said, filling the pot. "Siobhan, I wish you'd reconsider. You're risking eternal damnation for an evil man."

"Sister, I'm determined. Thanks for the food and the kind words."

"I'll pray that you don't do this. One favor—for me—come and see me before you carry this out."

"I will, Sister."

Siobhan and her Father

Siobhan O'Connor still thirsted for revenge. Half-drunk most of the time, her father was vaguely aware of her anger at him. She spoke to him only out of necessity. After simmering about the Palmerston attack for days, Siobhan exploded at her father: "You sold me for a crown to that man like I was a sheep in the field. He almost tore the backside off me. My sisters saw the whole thing. Is this how you will treat them too? This caravan is a traveling whorehouse. Then you go spend the money on Drink for yourself. You might as well drop me and the girls off in Dublin where streetwalkers at least get to keep the money from selling themselves. The girls and me would be better off on our own."

Shocked by his daughter's outburst, O'Connor said, "You mean you would leave us?"

"I want a life better than a whore's."

"Siobhan, I'm sorry about that man. He was well-dressed, rode a fine horse, and appeared a gentleman. I had no idea he would be so savage."

"Yes, but you did nothing when he raped me."

"Yes, Siobhan, but he had already paid me. I'm sorry, but what can I do about it now?"

"That man hurt me. I want revenge."

"All right then so, first we'll have a good look at his estate and get the lay of the land, like. We'll hide the caravan nearby and walk there," O'Connor said. "He's often out riding in the fields, so we'll have to keep a sharp eye out."

Mollified that her father had at least listened to her, Siobhan accompanied him. to the Palmerston house. As they got within two miles of the estate, they hid the caravan in the trees, covering it with trees and brush. The Cowper house stood high on a hill surrounded by meadows for grazing. Siobhan and her father crept through the field when Palmerston came riding toward them.

"Quick now, Siobhan, lay down in the long grass till they pass," O'Connor said. The riders came within a quarter of mile of them.

"Look at those fine fat sheep, Siobhan, good dinners for us." Two red barns flanked the back of the house with cattle lowing inside. When they had completed their circuit of the house, O'Connor said, "Well that's a good look for us." O'Connor tied three of the sheep with a rope and led them back to the caravan. O'Connor said, "The man with Palmerston seems no threat and there's only an old lady inside. In a few days we'll go directly to the house and offer to repair any pots and pans. The man will think you've come to have sex again and that will put him off his guard for us to steal sheep."

Dorset's Kindness

Out riding alone one afternoon, Dorset heard something shoot by his head, a stone the size of a teacup. He rode to the source of the missile and found a boy about twelve crying. The boy had a slingshot and a sack of dead rabbits by his side. Between sobs, the boy said, "I'm sorry, Sir. I meant no harm to you. I didn't see you and shot high."

"What are you doing on Mr. Palmerston's land? You can't hunt here."

"Me mam sent me out to get rabbits for our dinner. I won't come back again, I promise," the boy said.

"If the landlord caught you, it would mean a thrashing."

"Yes, Sir."

Handing the boy a crown from his pocket, Dorset said, "You can buy some food in town with this. If ever you need money for food, come to the back door of the house and see Mrs. O'Hearn who will fetch me, Jeremy Dorset, but you must avoid Mr. Palmerston at all costs."

Grateful for his escape and for the crown, the boy said, "God bless you, Mr. Dorset." He then scurried away across the field with his crown and sack of rabbits.

Dorset was pleased with himself because he had done a small kindness. It was a long time since someone had blessed him.

Maureen Mulcahy

It didn't take Palmerston long after his attack on Josie to renew his lust. Out riding by himself in the fields one afternoon, he spied a tall beauty with strawberry blond hair, Maureen Mulcahy, working alone hoeing a turnip patch. She caught his eye.

With no cottages nearby and no one else about, he had a clear chance to satisfy his lust for her. Riding behind her, Palmerston grabbed her by her peasant dress, which he tore away. He lost his balance and fell from his horse. Maureen's dress was in tatters. She eluded ran Palmerston's grasp, screaming, "Help! Help!" But there was no one to hear her.

When he continued to pursue her, screaming "I'll get you yet, you bitch Maureen turned to face him, grabbed her sharp spade, and with a running start lunged it into Palmerston's stomach wounding him badly. "You've killed me, you hoor."

A farmer, Bill Cassidy, was working in a field over the next hill and heard the girl's screams. Palmerston was lying unconscious where he landed. Cassidy rode to town to summon Sheriff Costello and Doctor Driscoll. When the two men arrived, the doctor said, "I can't patch him up here. He'll have to go to the hospital in Tralee."

For a second time the three men trundled Palmerston into Father Malloy's horse and trap. They brought him to Tralee. The surgeon in the hospital had to remove Palmerston's appendix and spleen, confining him to the hospital for weeks.

Dorset and Siobhan

When the tinkers reached Dingle to escape Palmerston for stealing his sheep, a farmer told them that the man was recuperating in the Tralee hospital. Paddy saw the opportunity to steal more sheep. Rather than taking the longer road through the Slieve Mish Mountains, the tinkers took the more direct route through Anascaul to Tralee, only seventeen miles from Listowel. Just to be on the safe side, the caravan traveled only on the back roads. Waiting until dark, the tinkers parked in a grove of trees near the Cowper Estate.

While Paddy and Tom stole six sheep, Siobhan entered the house by the back door. She met Jeremy Dorset coming from the sitting room. "What are you doing here? Oh, you're the girl whom Palmerston brutalized in the field," Dorset said.

"And you didn't lift a finger to stop him," Siobhan replied.

"Yes," he said, "I was a coward, under Palmerston's thumb. I've been sorry ever since. I remonstrated with him later, but it didn't do a bit of good."

"So now you're alone here with Palmerston in hospital."

"Yes," said Dorset, "but I've got a shotgun to defend myself with only the cattle and sheep to mind."

"Which my family are stealing right now."

"There are dozens of them," Dorset said. "You couldn't steal them all."

"Let me take a silver platter for my father as proof that I was in the house."

"Yes. I hope you come back to see me again."

Two days later with Palmerston in the hospital, Siobhan snuck into the Cowper house through the back door. She met Dorset in the sitting room enjoying a peat fire. He said, "Come sit by the fire and warm yourself. I can make some tea."

"No tea," she said. "I have to leave soon."

"What's life like for you as a traveler?" Dorset asked.

"Terrible, Sir. We never stay in one place for more than a few days. People hate us for our thieving, accuse us of polluting wells, and trampling their crops. In town young boys throw stones at us, and old women sprinkle us with holy water as if we're evil spirits."

"Have you ever thought about leaving the travelers?' Dorset asked.

"Every minute of every day. I almost left after your master assaulted me, but I have my mother and four young ones to care for."

"What about marriage?" Dorset asked.

"We're allowed to marry only other travelers in an arranged match. I'd have the same way of life as my mother, tied to a drunkard and wife beater. Why do you ask? Are you interested in me?" Siobhan asked.

"Very much."

"For a tumble?" Siobhan said.

"No," said Dorset, "if you'd have me, I'd like to marry you."

"But I don't even know your first name. I'm Siobhan O'Connor."

"Jeremy Dorset."

"You're a strange man," Siobhan said.

"I've loved you since the first day I set eyes on you. I'm trying to be a good man. I've been too shy to approach you, and Palmerston has ruled my life, but I'm going to break free of him. I must tell you that I'm a virgin, never been with a woman."

"That's learned easily enough," Siobhan said.

"Would you at least give marriage a think. I'd be kind to you."

"A welcome change," Siobhan said.

"I've written my father in Sheffield for a loan to build a cottage and farm to support us. I'll hear back in two weeks. Will you come back and see me again?"

"In a few days. I'll have to take something from the house for my father as an excuse for coming here," Siobhan said.

Looking around, in a cabinet Dorset saw a cut glass decanter that Palmerston wouldn't miss. "Would this do?" he asked.

"Perfect," Siobhan said and hurried out the door.

When she returned to the caravan, she gave the decanter to his father.

"Good," he said, "I can sell it in town."

Apology

Jeremy Dorset rode into Listowel and hobbled into the Mullins' knitting shop where Josie was wary of him.

Nervous, Dorset stammered, "Ms. Mullins, don't be afraid. I'm here to apologize for my cowardice at your hearing. I lied, doing you a terrible injustice. I've been under Palmerston's thumb, but that doesn't excuse my behavior. If you can find it in your heart to forgive me, I'd be most grateful."

"Mr. Dorset, I do forgive you. For a time I was very angry about the results of the trial, but I'm over the heartache. I know you have a hard life under Palmerston. I can only hope your life will be better in the future."

"I'll change my life in the future. Palmerston was kind to me for years, but he had grown steadily more brutal and lustful. I must break way from him. Thanks for your graciousness, Ms. Mullins. You're very kind."

Warning

After recuperating from his wounds, Palmerston returned to his estate. Sheriff Costello rode out to see him and criticized his behavior: "Mr. Palmerston, you've terrorized all the girls in the area, so much so that girls are afraid to walk alone on the roads. You must stop."

Palmerston retorted, "I'll act the way I want. Neither you nor anyone else can stop me."

"Palmerston, you're going to come to a bad end."

THREAT

After writing his father in Sheffield outlining his plans to build a farm and raise livestock, Jeremy asked for a loan to buy three acres of farmland from Lord Palmerston—always anxious for money. Lord Palmerston sold the land to Jeremy's father who mailed his son a signed contract for the land with additional money for buying cows, sheep, and pigs.

When Jeremy received the letter from his father, it was time for him to inform Palmerston who had just left the hospital that he would be leaving the Cowper Estate. Showing him the contract signed by Old Palmerston, Dorset said, "James, I've bought three acres of land from your father to build a cottage and carve out a farm close to it."

"What," Palmerston said, "you'd leave me after all I've done for you?"

"I want a life of my own. You've been kind to me, but this is something I'm going to do."

"So this is the thanks I get for bringing you over here, giving you a job, and providing you room and board for months."

"But I've worked hard for you tending the sheep and cattle and supervising the workers," Jeremy said.

"I'll bet this is over my tumbling of the Moore house or chasing the local girls. Who will take care of you " Palmerston asked.

"I'm going to marry and have a family."

"Who would marry you? You have no prospects," Palmerston said.

"My parents sent me money to purchase livestock from the locals and make my living. I've found someone to marry and that will be enough for me," Jeremy said.

"Who?"

"Siobhan O'Connor."

"You mean the tinker wench I took in the field one day?" Palmerton asked.

"Yes."

"You're a fool getting used goods," Palmerston said. "Besides, her father will never let her go as long as he can sell her for sex. All the world knows that a tinker will never stay with a settled man."

Jeremy said, "I'll stay with her and she with me."

"I thought you didn't even like sex. When I asked you if you wanted a tumble, you always refused. You don't even know how to have sex. You're a virgin, I'll wager. I took servant girls at fifteen when I was home."

"James, I don't like women the way you do, simply to force sex on them and then discard them. I can learn to love and be loved."

"Love," Palmerston scoffed. "There's no such thing--only lust and pleasure."

"We're different, James said. I'll live the way I wish."

"Your tinker bride won't stay long. I'll have another go at her myself. Show her a real man."

"She won't have you, and I'll stop you," Jeremy said.

"Don't be so sure. I enjoyed her once, and I will again."

SIOBHAN'S REVOLT

On the road one day, a middle-aged farmer on a gray horse and wearing dirty work clothes stopped the caravan. "I like the cut of your driver. How much for a coupling with the girl?" he asked O'Connor pointing to Siobhan.

"A crown," O'Connor said.

"Fair enough," the man said, pulling a crown from his purse.

Siobhan said to her father, "You'll sell me no more."

"But that's a crown," her father said.

"I won't do it."

"You've never refused before," O'Connor said

"I won't do it."

"It's either you give the man a tumble or you get a good hiding," her father said.

After the farmer went away disappointed, O'Connor dragged his daughter from the van, took off his belt, and lay ten stripes across her back. "Next time you'll do as you're told."

Shedding no tears, Siobhan said, "I will not."

O'Connor was in a quandary. He was the chief, the father, and his eldest had disobeyed him.

The next day the tinkers stopped to beg for food at St. Michael's. Anxious to speak with Sister Clare, Siobhan grabbed the empty pot and headed for the kitchen where the nun was stirring a pot of vegetable soup. "Siobhan," the nun said, "I haven't seen you for weeks. Let's have some tea."

"If it's no trouble, Sister."

Something about Siobhan was different. She had a glow about her, but physically she moved slowly and slid into her chair with some difficulty.

"Does your back hurt?" the nun asked.

"Yes," Siobhan answered. "My father whipped me for refusing sex with a farmer."

"Well, let's tend to your wounds first. The tea can wait."

Going upstairs, the nun cleaned the wounds and rubbed salve on her cuts. Returning to the kitchen, Sister Clare made more tea.

"Sister, besides coming for food, I want to ask your advice, but it must remain secret."

"I can keep secrets," the nun said.

"Jeremy Dorset, who lives at the Cowper Estate has asked me to marry him, and I want to."

"What does your family say?" Sister Clare asked.

"I haven't told them. My father will be furious. I can live with that, but I'll miss my mother and the children."

"Isn't Dorset disabled with a club foot?" the nun asked.

"Yes, but he makes his way around with a cane."

"What type of man is he?" the nun asked.

"Kind and gentle, though he has acquired a bad reputation from living with Palmerston."

"With his disability will he be able to support you?" Sister Clare asked.

"He's hoping to buy a small farm with a loan from his family in England. He's good with livestock and can supervise workers, which he learned from Palmerston. And he's willing to convert to the Catholic Church to marry me." Though finished with her tea, Siobhan kept on talking. "Sister, what do you think?"

"You must follow your heart. If you love the man and can live with your father's disapproval, go ahead and marry him. There's no law against a traveler marrying a settled man."

"Sister, pray for me that I have the courage to do this," Siobhan said.

"I will. God bless you."

"The nun filled the pot with the soup for the caravan.

Siobhan left with Sister Clare's blessing. She had gained more confidence from speaking with her.

"What took you so long?" Siobhan's father growled when she returned to the caravan.

"The soup had to cool."

"No tricks, Siobhan, or else I'll beat you again."

Siobhan was planning the biggest trick of all—leaving the band of travelers.

Later that week when Siobhan was able to sneak away from the caravan, Dorset gave her the good news: His parents had loaned him the money to buy his farm. "Siobhan, will you marry me?" he asked.

"Yes."

"We have to see Father Malloy as St. Michael's for my baptism to convert to your church and arrange for our marriage. Later I'll ask Sean Kavanagh to help me choose three acres for our farm."

"I'm thrilled, Jeremy. A chance to live the way we wish."

"From the first time I saw you, I knew you were the woman for me. I love you."

"Jeremy, give me something to bring back as my excuse for being here."

He gave her a silver spoon. "Hopefully, this is the last thing I ever steal from here," Siobhan said.

Siobhan knew that the hardest part was yet to come, confronting her father and leaving her mother and the little ones. In the end she decided to sneak away from the caravan, but not without telling her mother.

One afternoon when Paddy went to the Harp and Shamrock pub in Listowel, Siobhan pulled her mother aside and told of her plans: "Mam, I'm going to leave the band and marry a settled man, Jeremy Dorset."

"Good," her mother said, "but I'll miss you terribly. I've been on the road all me life, and I've had me fill of it and your father. Now you can have a real life. I won't say a word to him. Mind you don't let any of this slip to him".

"I won't, Mam."

"He'll be off his head but will eventually have to give up and move on," Sally said. "The children will miss you too, but this is for the best." Mother and daughter held each tightly, both of them crying.

Dorset's Baptism

Accompanied by Sister Clare and Sean Kavanagh, Jeremy and Siobhan followed Father Malloy into the church for the baptism. The nun and Sean Kavanagh would be the godparents for Jeremy. They walked to the stone baptismal font at the front of the church, a lit candle on the altar beside it.

Father Malloy began the ancient formula: "I baptize you in the name of Father, Son, and Holy Ghost," tracing the Sign of the Cross with holy water on Jeremy's head.

The couple thanked Father Malloy who said, "Normally, I'd announce the banns of your marriage on Sunday, but it's better for Siobhan if we keep this secret for now until her family departs. We'll hold the marriage on Sunday afternoon when Sister Clare and Sean will stand up for you as witnesses."

WEDDING

The following Sunday afternoon was bright and sunny, a perfect day for a wedding. Siobhan felt bad that her mother and the little ones would not be present at the ceremony, but her father had made that impossible. Mary Kavanagh gave Siobhan her own wedding dress, not overly long with a lace top.

Father Malloy began the wedding ritual:

"My dear friends, you have come together in this church so that the Lord may seal and strengthen your love in the presence of the Church's minister and this community. Christ abundantly blesses this love. He has already consecrated you in baptism and now he enriches and strengthens you by a special sacrament so that you may assume the duties of marriage in mutual and lasting fidelity. And so, in the presence of the Church, I ask you to state your intentions."

"Siobhan and Jeremy, have you come here freely and without reservation to give yourselves to each other in marriage?"

"Yes, Father," they both answered.

"Will you love and honor each other as man and wife for the rest of your lives?"

"Yes," they said

"Will you accept children lovingly from God and bring them up according to the law of Christ and his Church?"

"Yes, Father," they replied.

"Since it is your intention to enter into marriage, join your right hands, and declare your consent before God and his Church."

"Jeremy and Siobhan join hands and exchange rings."

"I, Jeremy, take you, Siobhan, to be my wife. I promise to be true to you in good times and in bad, in sickness and in health. I will love you and honor you all the days of my life."

"I, Siobhan, take you, Jeremy, to be my husband. I promise to be true to you in good times and in bad, in sickness and in health. I will love you and honor you all the days of my life."

Sister Clare had bought two rings from the sale of her own knitting and had given them to the couple that morning. Jeremy promised to repay her.

Father Malloy concluded the wedding:

"You have declared your consent before the Church. May the Lord in his goodness strengthen your consent and fill you both with his blessings. What God has joined, men must not divide."

The Dorsets soon became friends with the Kavanaghs who had been so kind to them. Over tea at Sean and Mary's house, Jeremy brought out the contract for three acres from Lord Palmerston that his parents had purchased. "Sean," Jeremy said, "would you help me choose a good piece of land for a cottage and farm, some distance from the Cowper house. I'd also like to buy two good sheepdogs from you that would double as watchdogs."

Sean agreed and said, "I have two young border collies that I've trained myself."

The next day Sean and Jeremy looked at several sites, choosing one atop a small hill with a narrow tributary of the River Feale running behind it, flat lands below it for farming. In time he would raise sheep and cows. "Sean," Jeremy asked, "would you help me choose some men to build us a cottage on one floor with no stairs so I could get around easily and later put up a barn close by?"

"That's easily done," said Sean, "after the harvest when men would love a job."

"I have money to pay them, and I can supervise the work, one good thing I learned from Palmerston. I'm also good with animals, so I need to buy some livestock."

'That's no problem, Jeremy. I know the farmers well, and they'd sell you healthy animals."

Siobhan loved visiting the Kavanagh house and playing with the children. The only ache in her heart was missing the little ones from her own family. As an outcast she feared that she might never see them again, but she had resolved not to be a traveler. She told Mary Kavanagh, "I want to be a settled woman, a tinker no more."

In their marriage, Jeremy and Siobhan were thriving. Siobhan introduced her husband to lovemaking in which he was gentle unlike his master. They both wanted children, but Jeremy feared that one of their children might inherit his disability of a clubfoot. Siobhan said to him, "None of your siblings has a clubfoot. You told me Palmerston's didn't either, so let us put our trust in God that our babies be healthy."

Ten months after their marriage, Jeremy and Siobhan had a healthy little girl with Mary Kavanagh serving as midwife. The couple named the baby Sally in honor of Siobhan's mother. Neighboring laborers built their cottage of local stone, with mortar filling any cracks, and a thatched roof. Much of the stone came from the River Feale close by. With three windows in front, the cottage was bright.

Father Malloy baptized the baby, the Kavanaghs serving as godparents.

After talking with Mary about the danger from O'Connor, John asked what she thought. "Why don't you confront the devil—the sheriff, and you, with Siobhan and Jeremy? What about the mother?"

"Siobhan told me the poor woman tried to drown herself in the River Feale. But, Mary, your idea is a good one because the tinkers are afraid of the sheriff."

John rode the few miles to the Dorset farm where he was always welcome. The look on John's face, however, indicated he was bearing bad news. He said to Jeremy and Siobhan: "Your father had been sneaking around here and has found where you live. We're afraid he's coming for you, Siobhan." She took the news calmly.

Sean said, "You don't seem surprised or upset. I thought this would put the heart crossways in you."

"No," she said, "whatever love I had for my father he drove out long ago."

"What of your mother?" John asked.

"She only wants what is best for me, never again to be a traveler. My father has broken her—almost. If my father comes, we have the dogs and a shotgun, which Jeremy has taught me to use. This is my family now. If he comes here, either of us would shoot him."

"Mary had an idea, Siobhan—to confront him with you both, me, and the sheriff, At the very least, it would be a warning to him, like. Do you think it would do any good?"

"No."

"We could at least give it a try," Jeremy said.

"My father is an evil man, especially with the Drink on him—which is most of the time," Siobhan said. "But if you're determined we can make the attempt."

Sean said, "I'll see the sheriff who already knows the danger."

"We'll take the baby. Me Ma and the little ones should see her. The best time to go is in the early morning before he begins his day's drinking."

CONFRONTATION

Early the next morning under gray lowering skies, Sheriff Driscoll, Sean Kavanagh, Jeremy, and Siobhan with baby Sally rode the six miles to where O'Connor had made camp in a grove of trees off Listowel Road. Before they reached the caravan, the group could smell smoke and the horses. Her mother and the children came running for hugs and kisses as soon as they saw Siobhan. Afraid of offending his father, Tom hung back.

"This is baby Sally, Mam, your grandchild," handing the infant wrapped in a blue woolen blanket to her mother and then to the little girls.

"God bless her, she's beautiful," Sally said.

"Like you, Mam," Siobhan said, "and she has your name. This is my husband Jeremy, our friend Sean Kavanagh, and Sheriff Driscoll. We need to speak with my father."

Returning to the van, Sally shook Paddy O'Connor from sleep. Sally said, "You have visitors. Wake up."

"Who?"

"Come and see," Sally said.

Groggy from sleep and last night's drinking, O'Connor stumbled from the caravan. Seeing Siobhan, O'Connor asked, "You've come back to us so?"

"No, never again."

"Who is this gang you've brought against me?" O'Connor asked.

"My husband Jeremy, our baby Sally, Sean Kavanagh, and the sheriff you know."

Seeing the baby, O'Connor asked, "This is your little bastard?"

"She's no bastard. We're married and she's been baptized."

"Your husband is only half a man, to be sure," O'Connor said.

"He's more a man than you've ever were," Siobhan said.

"Why have you come here?" O'Connor asked.

86

"To warn you off, O'Connor," the sheriff interjected. "I'll jail you if you keep prowling around here. I want you gone."

"On what grounds?"

"Vagrancy," the sheriff said.

"You mean I can't travel these roads."

"Not these roads. If you aren't gone by tomorrow morning, I'll put you in jail," the sheriff said.

"You can't do this," O'Connor said.

"Watch me," the sheriff replied.

"Siobhan, you would do this to your own father?"

"You stopped being my father years ago when you beat me and sold me as a prostitute."

O'Connor turned red in the face. "What of your mother and the little ones?"

"I'm sorry for them, but when the children are grown they can do what I did," Siobhan said.

O'Connor said, "From now on I pronounce a curse upon you and yours. You're an outcast."

"That's what I want," Siobhan said, "to escape you and your evil."

The little group turned toward the Listowel Road and headed for home. Her mother and little sisters cried at her going. For her part, Siobhan was sad to leave them, but at least they had seen baby Sally.

Paddy O'Connor spent the rest of the day sucking on his poitin and beating Sally who knew his black heart. She resolved that if he carried Siobhan back to the band, she would kill him, God forgive her. She was sure He would.

That night with the children asleep, Sean and Mary discussed the visit to the caravan. Mary asked, "Is there any decency in the man at all?"

"No, he's a drunk and a wife-beater. Siobhan did right to leave. I feel sorry for the mother and the little ones"

"What's the wife like, Sean?"

"A poor long-suffering tinker mother. Siobhan told me the mother in despair tried to drown herself in the River Feale after Palmerston raped and abused the girl last year. A fisherman pulled the mother out. But despite her troubles, the mother is determined that Siobhan stay free."

"Mother of God, what a life, Mary said, "always on the road begging for food. The children have no education. They'd be better off at St. Michael's where at least they could get schooling."

"Yes."

"Do you think the father will leave Siobhan in peace?"

"Mary, I don't know. He's a very bad man—even for a tinker. I don't trust him at all at all."

At home Jeremy and Siobhan talked of their visit to the caravan. Jeremy asked Siobhan, "Do you think he'll leave us alone?"

"No," Siobhan said. "Despite the curse he put on me, he wants to drag me back."

"What can we do, love?" Jeremy asked.

"We both have to steel ourselves for the worst. I know your nature is kind; but if my father returns, he wants only one thing—me. We have to defend our family and shoot him, something neither of us wants."

The Whiteboys

Arrest of a Molly Maguire (Whiteboy)

One stormy evening as Sean and little Joseph were herding their sheep into the barn, six men dressed in white smocks and wearing masks accosted them. Sean knew immediately they were Whiteboys.

"What's your name?" the leader asked.

"Why do you want to know?" Sean replied.

"We ask the questions. You answer them, or else it will go bad for your family."

"Sean Kavanagh."

"Who's your landlord?"

"I don't have one. I own this farm."

The leader asked, "Do you know who we are?"

"I can guess."

"We're here to stop poor tenants from paying rents to greedy landlords," the leader said.

"More power to you," Sean said. "But the local landlord Palmerston died in an accident two weeks ago."

"Tell me, Kavanagh, are there any dragoons about?"

"They have a barracks seventeen miles east of us in Tralee."

"Have they ever bothered you?" the leader asked.

Sean answered, "No, but they tumbled and burned down the cottage of my neighbor Michael Moore."

"How did they act?'

"Like most English dragoons—cold, haughty, unconcerned with the Moores whom they were evicting."

"Kavanagh, you seem a strong, principled man. Do you wish to join us in our work?"

"No, I have five little ones to raise and this farm to maintain."

"Don't you want to protect your children for the future? That's our work," the leader said.

"I'll protect my own," Sean said.

"'Sean Kavanagh'—that name triggers a memory from a story I heard in Dingle. Did you change your name from 'John Kevane' and shoot landlord Mahon in Dingle years ago?" asked the leader.

"No," Sean lied. "I was born and raised in Listowel. The landlord tumbled our house, and I became an orphan at St. Michael's just down the road."

"I'm not sure I believe your story. You're too clever by half. We have to visit the tenants on the Cowper Estate, and then I'll check your story."

As the Whiteboys rode east, Sean raced his horse west to St. Michael's to consult Father Malloy and Sister Clare.

When Sean reached St. Michael's, he asked Sister Clare to join him in the rectory while he spoke with Father Malloy. He told them his account which both of them had already known. "The Whiteboys want to impress me into their service by blackmailing me about shooting Major Mahon. I told them I was born and raised in Listowel and grew up here as an orphan. I need you both to verify my tale."

"That's no problem, Sean," Father Malloy said. "We'll tell the Whiteboys the same story. As if we haven't enough trouble with the English, we have our own mischief-makers."

Sister Clare agreed: "I'll repeat your account. The past is past, and you're a good man."

As it was growing dusk, the Whiteboys rode back on Listowel Road. They knocked on the rectory door and met Father Malloy who was reading his breviary, the daily prayer for priests. "Father," the leader said, "I believe that one of your parishioners, Sean Kavanagh, is living here under an assumed name. He really is 'Johnjoe Kevane' who murdered Major Mahon."

"Your belief is wrong. Kavanagh was a child here in Listowel and grew up in our orphanage across the road."

"Father, who is in charge of the orphanage?"

"I am, but Sister Clare, a Mercy nun, actually runs the place, God love her."

While the other five Whiteboys ambled back and forth in front of the school on their horses, the leader entered the orphanage to find Sister Clare who was teaching ten young girls upstairs in the knitting room.

"Who are you and why do you wear masks?" Sister Clare asked. "You're scaring the children."

"We're Whiteboys and wear masks to protect our identities. But I'm here on another matter". Trying to trick Sister Clare, the leader said, "I'm trying to find Johnjoe Kevane who attended this orphanage."

"You're mistaken. He never came here."

"What of Sean Kavanagh?" the leader asked.

"Yes, he came here as an orphan when his parents died. I helped raise him."

"Sister, I hope you've been truthful with me," the leader said.

"I am."

When Sean returned home before the Whiteboys could know he had been at St. Michael's, he told Mary the story. "The Whiteboys tried to force me to join them by holding 'Johnjoe Kevane' and the Mahon shooting over my head."

"Will they ever leave us in peace," Mary replied. "We're till fighting Palmerston, and now these devils come to trouble us."

"I talked to Father Malloy and Sister Clare to cover for me. And these men avoid towns like Listowel for fear of the sheriff and dragoons. None of the farmers here knows my history, so we're safe."

"Thank God," Mary replied.

ATTACK ON THE WHITEBOYS

The Whiteboys stayed in the area east of Listowel for several weeks, journeying as far south as Abbeyfeale and as far north as Tarbert. They had threatened Jim Kelly, a farmer from neighboring Lissaniska, who rode to Listowel to inform Sheriff Driscoll who in his turn traveled through a driving rain to Tralee and informed Captain Davison of the dragoons: "There's a gang of Whiteboys about, at least six, harassing tenants near the Cowper lands ".

"Thanks for the news, Sheriff. We'll be right out after them."

Six dragoons with muskets, sabers, and pistols were more than a match for the Whiteboys, hiding in a camp just south of the Cowper lands. Spreading themselves out among the trees, the dragons cut off any escape route. Captain Davison rode into the middle of the group announcing, "You're all under arrest!"

Most of the Whiteboys scattered into the woods where the dragoons captured them, but the leader with his pistol shot the captain high in the chest as another dragoon came with his bayonet and thrust it through the shooter.

Davison remembered that Sean Kavanagh lived just off Listowel Road where he directed his men to bring him. Lieutenant Raftery, the second in command, tied the captain's horse to his and arrived the Kavanagh home. The dragoons knocked on the door. Mary answered but Sean was in town. When she asked Raftery what had happened, he said, "Shot by the Whiteboys, Missus. I haven't inspected his wound, but he's lost much blood. He is in and out of consciousness."

"Well, bring him in," Mary said, laying some blankets on the floor. "Put him near the fire." Unbuttoning his tunic, Mary saw that the bullet had hit Davison high in the chest but had missed his heart and lungs. One of you men get Dr. Driscoll from Listowel to see the wound, but you may have to transport him to a proper hospital in Tralee. Father Malloy has a horse and trap you can take him in."

By this time Sean Kavanagh had returned home and went to fetch Father Malloy's horse and buggy. Sean recruited Sister Clare to ride with Davison to make him comfortable with blankets and some tea in a pitcher. The other four dragoons brought the captive Whiteboys to Sheriff Driscoll for jail. Weakened by his wound and only half-conscious, Davison asked Sister Clare "Where are we going?"

"To the hospital in Tralee, Captain," Sister Clare said.

"Where are my men?"

Sister Clare said "Your lieutenant is riding beside you, and the rest are bringing the remaining Whiteboys to jail. Hush now, no more questions. You must save your strength"

News travels fast in a small town. A mile west of Listowel, four farmers carrying pitchforks blocked the road. A middle-aged farmer with a face the color of strawberries, said, "We heard the dragoons attacked some Whiteboys."

Lieutenant Raftery said, "Yes."

"Any deaths?"

"The Whiteboy who shot the captain," Raftery said.

Turning to Sean Kavanagh, the farmer asked, "Where are you taking this dragoon captain?"

"To the hospital in Tralee."

"Sure, isn't he the man who presided over the tumbling of the Moore cottage?" asked the farmer.

"Yes."

"Well then let's finish him off right here," the farmer said.

"No," Sean said, "he's gravely wounded. That would be murder."

"I don't care," said the farmer. "There are four of us and only two of ye. Only the one dragoon is armed."

"That means at least two of you will meet your Maker, and there are four more dragoons riding up behind us," Sean said.

"Aren't you a farmer?" the man asked Sean.

"Yes."

"And here you are protecting one of our enemy," the farmer said.

"This is common humanity to help an injured man," Sean said. "Even Our Lord helped the sick and dying."

"I hope these dragoons tumble your house some day," said the farmer. "You may not feel so compassionate then."

With that the four farmers melted into the woods alongside the road.

"Thanks," said Lieutenant Raftery. "You may have saved the captain's life today."

Captain Davison suffered a broken collarbone and bled heavily. After spending six weeks in the hospital and wearing a sling, he returned to the barracks for a rest of three days. On the fourth day he set out from his quarters under a soft rain. He had a mission. Back in uniform, he sought Sean Kavanagh, taking the Listowel Road under a canopy of dripping oak trees. Having been at the Kavanagh house twice before, he found their cottage easily. Sean and his son Joseph were herding the ten sheep into the barn. Sean would sell their wool at cost to Josie Mullins for her shop in town.

As the captain approached, Sean hailed him. "I'm glad to see you on the mend."

"Thanks to you," the captain said.

"It was the Christian thing to do, and your lieutenant put the fear of God into those farmers, " Sean said.

"He told me about your courage in facing those men. I'm grateful. I know you hold the Moore tumbling against me, but it was sad duty for us too. I'm Catholic as are several of my men. We do not enjoy tearing down the homes of these tenants. Sadly we are under orders from our masters. I hope that soon London will put an end to it. I fought the Punjabs in India and would rather be doing that than hurting your people."

"I understand, Captain."

"The Whiteboys are a different matter because they hurt us all, especially the poor farmers whom they browbeat to join them."

"Yes, they tried to force me also," Sean said.

"If I can ever can do anything for you, please ask. As I said, you helped save my life."

"Captain, why don't you drop in and have a cup to tea before you go on the road again?"

Pleased by the offer, the captain accepted, and Sean went inside to tell Mary to put the kettle on. A peat fire burned in the hearth. "Sit close to the fire, Captain," Mary said, "to take the chill off, like." Four little girls and Joseph were playing in the kitchen, and Davison enjoyed watching their games.

"I have two little girls of my own back in Chester. Would I were there," the captain said.

"What are their names," Mary asked

"Emily four and Sarah three. My wife is Anna. I haven't seen them in two years. Mrs. Kavanagh, thanks for your kindness."

"In these times we could all use some charity," Mary said.

"Amen to that. I wish these terrible times were over—for all of us. And now there is a possibility of new troubles. Our government in London would like to join the Confederates in the American Civil War, all for money from the cotton trade. We've already made and sent over three ships to the Rebels to break the Union blockade of cotton ships. Lord Palmerston, father of James, is negotiating secretly with the South—as if we didn't have our hands full in India."

"Yes," Sean said, "the North has sent over Irishmen to recruit for their cause, and with no jobs many men are joining them."

After a second helping of tea with buttermilk biscuits, the captain said, "I'd best be going. My men will think I've deserted them."

Sean said, "Captain, I'd like to accompany you through the end of Listowel town and a mile or so farther just to guard against any more farmers."

"I will be glad of your company. It will make the ride more pleasant," the captain said.

As they passed St. Michael's, Davison said, "Give my thanks to Father Malloy and Sister Clare. She covered me with blankets to keep me warm on the ride to Tralee."

"I will."

Sean rode with the captain through town and a mile beyond, people gawping at the strange sight of a farmer, one of their own, escorting a dragoon captain.

TRAGEDY

As the sheriff had ordered, the caravan moved east close to Tralee when tragedy struck. One morning camped outside the city, Sally plaited the long dark hair of her youngest, Eileen, and sent her out to play. The little girl was gone but an hour when her son Tom came running to his mother crying, "Eileen is stuck in some long grass by the river, and I can't pull her out. Come help me."

Sally ran to the riverbank with Tom only to find her daughter dead, drowned in a few feet of water. "Oh, my poor dead daughter," Sally screamed. She couldn't tell Paddy because he was off drinking.

That night the family buried the little girl in a nearby field, Sally howling and throwing herself on the grave. Unusual for her, she became drunk and swallowed ashes and white paint as a sign of mourning. The death of her little girl gave Sally one more reason to hate her husband. Had he not driven Siobhan away, her eldest daughter would have been home to mind the little ones, and Eileen might still be alive.

Having heard the terrible news, Jeremy told Siobhan of Eileen's death. Siobhan burst into hysterics. "If I had been there, this wouldn't have happened," she told Jeremy. Not a little of her sorrow was guilt over abandoning the caravan and giving up her role as protector of the children. "Jeremy, I'm going to ride to see Sister Clare."

Siobhan brought her troubles to the nun: "Sister, if I had been there, Eileen might not have drowned."

The nun told her "You've been a good sister to Eileen. You made the right decision to leave the band, didn't you?"

"Yes, Sister."

"Eileen's death is a tragedy," said Sister Clare. "We don't know God's ways in allowing her death, but you shouldn't blame yourself over something over which you had no control. Your father could have been there as was Tom was and your mother."

"Yes, Sister, but Eileen's death still stings."

"Of course because you loved her. Father Malloy will say a Mass tomorrow morning for Eileen and your family."

"Thanks, Sister. You're always a help to me."

EDUCATION

A few weeks after their marriage, Siobhan came to St. Michael's to see Sister Clare. "Sister," she said, "I want to learn how to knit. I have some money to pay for the instruction."

"Girl, keep your money. We have a class in knitting every day." So Siobhan began to learn knitting, which would be a big help when Jeremy's sheep began producing wool. She caught on fast. The other girls in the class of eight were orphaned daughters of farmers who had died or been evicted. Because Siobhan had been a traveler, she endured gibes and taunts from the other girls—until Sister Clare put a stop to all the insults when she walked into the class and heard them one morning. Red-faced and angry, the nun said, "Now that's enough of that! Sure, you're all in the same boat learning a craft to support yourselves like the Mullins' sisters with their shop in Listowel. I'll have no more unkind comments, mind."

One afternoon after class, Siobhan came into the kitchen at St. Michael's, "Sister, I have no education. I know me catechism and letters from me Mam, but I've never been to school. Sure Jeremy is always reading at home, and I'm as dumb as a stone."

Sister Clare brought out some early reading books, "primers," and she started in with Siobhan right away. "We'll work an hour every afternoon after knitting, and Jeremy can help you at home."

Jeremy was a patient tutor who had learned from demanding taskmasters in England. Starting with the Bible, Jeremy introduced her to Bunyan's *Pilgrim's Progress*, a dense book but a good place to start.

After several days of buying drinks in the Cork and Kerry pub in Listowel, Paddy O'Connor learned from his companions that Siobhan and Dorset had built a cottage and farm several miles north of the Cowper house. One afternoon telling Sally he was going to Listowel, Paddy took a horse and scouted the farm and the land around it. Sally suspected her husband of more deviltry and told Tom to follow him at distance to see what his father was up to. When Tom saw his father turn from the road to Listowel, and head for the Cowper Estate, he was sure trouble would follow.

A few miles into the Cowper lands, Paddy found a new cottage with a barn alongside it. He stayed far enough away that his father couldn't see him. Dorset was tending sheep in a pasture, helped by a laborer walking beside him. No other cottages stood near, an ideal place for Paddy to snatch back Siobhan. The caravan could never cross the dense pastures, so he would have to grab her on horseback. About the baby he didn't care.

Some half a mile away, Tom observed the scene and raced back to his mother: "Mam, Da has found the cottage where Siobhan lives."

Unsurprised by the news, Sally made plans of her own. When Paddy went to the Harp and Shamrock in town, she left Tom in charge of the little ones and walked to St. Michael's. She knocked on the back door and met Sister Clare who was in the kitchen making supper. "Sister, I'm Sally O'Connor, Siobhan's mother. I know you've helped her a great deal, and I've come for your advice."

"Well," said Sister Clare, "Let's sit and have some tea."

While drinking their tea, Sally told the nun her worries: "I'm afraid that my husband, the devil, wants to capture Siobhan and return her as a traveler. He's been scouting her cottage. "At least twice he's been nosing around her farm."

Sister Clare told Sean Kavanagh about the threat from O'Connor. Sean would alert the sheriff and the local farmers to be on the lookout for him. Sean asked if he should inform Jeremy and Siobhan to be on their guard, "Sure they've lived in peace over a year and been to Mass every Sunday with their baby." Sister Clare and Father Malloy both agreed that Sean should warn the Dorsets, a task for which he was not anxious.

Mary's Advice

After talking with Mary about the danger from O'Connor, Sean asked what she thought. "Why don't you confront the devil—the sheriff, and you, with Siobhan and Jeremy? What about the mother?"

"Siobhan told me the poor woman tried to drown herself in the River Feale. But, Mary, your idea is a good one because the tinkers are afraid of the sheriff."

Sean rode the few miles to the Dorset farm where he was always welcome. The look on Sean's face, however, indicated he was bearing bad news. He said to Jeremy and Siobhan: "Your father had been sneaking around here and has found where you live. We're afraid he's coming for you, Siobhan." She took the news calmly.

Sean said, "You don't seem surprised or upset. I thought this would put the heart crossways in you."

"No," she said, "whatever love I had for my father he drove out long ago."

"What of your mother?" Sean asked.

"She only wants what is best for me, never again to be a traveler. My father has broken her—almost. If my father comes, we have the dogs and a shotgun, which Jeremy has taught me to use. This is my family now. If he comes here, either of us would shoot him."

"Mary had an idea, Siobhan—to confront him with you both, me, and the sheriff. At the very least, it would be a warning to him, like. Do you think it would do any good?"

"No."

"We could at least give it a try," Jeremy said.

"My father is an evil man, especially with the Drink on him—which is most of the time," Siobhan said. "But if you're determined we can make the attempt."

Sean said, "I'll see the sheriff who already knows the danger."

"We'll take the baby. Me Ma and the little ones should see her. The best time to go is in the early morning before he begins his day's drinking."

That evening Jeremy asked Siobhan, "Are you afraid of facing your father?'

"No," she said. "You and I are bound together forever. My father can't change that."

After several days of buying drinks in the Cork and Kerry pub in Listowel, Paddy O'Connor learned from his companions that Siobhan and Dorset had built a cottage and farm several miles north of the Cowper house. One afternoon telling Sally he was going to Listowel, Paddy took a horse and scouted the farm and the land around it. Sally suspected her husband of more deviltry and told Tom to follow him distance to see what his father was up to. When Tom saw his father turn from the road to Listowel, and head for the Cowper Estate, he knew trouble would follow.

THE QUAKERS

"The Society of Friends did much to stay the plague and their work was carried on by volunteers who asked no reward. . . .[The Quakers] spent no time in idle commenting on the Protestant or Papist faith, the Radical, Whig, or Tory politics, but looked at things as they were and faithfully recorded what they saw. . . . they relieved, they talked and wrote, but acted more. As I followed in their wake through the country the name of 'blessed William Forster' was on the lips of the poor cabiners. . . . When the question was put 'Who feeds you, or Who sent you these clothes, the answer was 'the good Quakers lady and they that have the religion entirely'."

Asenath Nicholson (multitext.ucc.ie/d/).
Asenath Nicholson, American philanthropist and caregiver.
www.famineghost.com

Over a million people starved in Ireland during The Great Hunger (1845-1850); more than a two million more fled the country in "coffin ships" when the English destroyed their cottages and farms. The suffering would have been even worse except for the Quakers. During the Famine, the Quakers studied the destitution in the west of Ireland, and Joseph Bewley, a successful Dublin businessman, who operated tea and coffee shops, founded the Society of Friends Central Relief Committee which purchased 294 copper steam vats at cost from the Quaker firm of Albert Darby in Liverpool. The Quakers distributed the boilers to workhouses and their own soup kitchens throughout Ireland for cooking "stirabout," a mixture of corn maize and rice that they had imported from the South where the Society had to overcome their aversion to slavery. They founded schools taught by Quaker women to teach children reading and writing, net mending, quilting and lace making. In agriculture the Quakers established a working model farm in Colmanstown, Galway, to teach 350 Irish farmers

Sean Kavanagh among them how to raise cows, pigs, and other livestock as well as how to cultivate wheat, turnips, cabbage, and other vegetables. For the fishing industry, the Friends persuaded the Admiralty to chart the rocky waters around the coasts, which had never been done before. They also improved fishing at Ring and Ballycotton by setting up curing houses and by providing clothes for fishermen out on the ocean. Most importantly, the Quakers spoke to Parliament and Prime Minister John Russell about the starvation and deaths in Ireland. No private group in Ireland did as much for the starving Irish as the Quakers.

A man dressed in plain brown pants and jacket, a Quaker, Thomas Pim, was driving a wagon full of wheat and rice to St. Michael's, a place he had visited many times. Although the Quakers had halted much of their relief work because of the parsimony of Great Britain, they still occasionally furnished what supplies they could to outlying areas, including poor houses, orphanages, and institutions that they knew used the food well.

Sister Clare was glad to see Mr. Pim again and walked him across the road for tea with Father Malloy before the man had to make the return trip to Dublin. In the meantime, schoolboys unloaded the food. "Welcome, Mr. Pim," the priest said. "You're still carrying on the work of Mr. Bewley, my dear friend for years. He saved many poor Irish with his supplies of food, even in Skibbereen, the most diseased part of Ireland."

"I miss him too," Pim said. "He was the kindest of us, finally dying of exhaustion from all his labors. Eleven more Quakers died of famine-related diseases too."

Sister Clare asked, "What work are ye involved in now?"

"We petition Parliament for more help to Ireland, such as keeping our produce here instead of sending it off to England. Poor Daniel O'Connell made the same plea to Parliament, but the ministers ignored him."

"He died not long after," said Father Malloy.

'In all, fifteen Quakers have died of famine-related diseases."

"The only real long-term solution is for the Irish to own their own land, not these English aristocrats who don't even live here,' Pim said.

Sister Clare said, "Ireland has much to thank ye Quakers for. You've helped the fishing industry by loaning men money to redeem their boats and equipment from pawn, by training women and children to sew nets, and by getting the English admiralty to chart our seas."

Father Malloy added "Your model farm on Colmanstown has trained hundreds of young Irish farmers to diversify their crops rather than depending on the potato. There are 3000 of ye in our population of 8 and a half million. You've done wonders, even buying copper vats to cook soup, and purchasing fishing tackle, seeds, and farm implements."

Mr. Pim explained, "Right now we are facing a crisis of conscience in the American Civil War. Many of our members have answered President Lincoln's call for enlistment in the Union Army. It's a paradox: We oppose war, but we've decided to end war and slavery by fighting against the South. In a eulogy for a fallen Quaker soldier, one of our ministers said that 'war as an all-consuming evil created by slavery that caused men to engage in evil in order to destroy evil.'" Mark A. Schmidt *"Patriotism and Paradox: Quaker Military Service in the American Civil War.*

"I only wish the hierarchy of the Church of England would do more for us than collect tithes, and our own church do more than engage in politics with Great Britain in the vain hope that they restore ties with the Vatican," said Father Malloy. "They did raise over 400,000 pounds thanks to Archbishop McHale and Archbishop Murray. The Americans donated more than $2,000,000. Even the Queen gave us 2000 pounds."

Sister Clare thanked Pim for the food: "You've been a Godsend to us all these years."

When two boys had unloaded the food, Mr. Pim set out for his return trip to Dublin with the praise and thanks of Father Malloy and Sister Clare ringing in his ears.

THE CORK SOCIETY OF FRIENDS' SOUP HOUSE.
Soup Kitchen Run by the Quakers

STEVE TAYLOR VIEWS OF THE FAMINE

Paddy's Search

After several days of buying drinks in the Cork and Kerry pub in Listowel, Paddy O'Connor learned from his companions that Siobhan and Dorset had built a cottage and farm several miles north of the Cowper house. One afternoon telling Sally he was going to Listowel, Paddy took a horse and scouted the farm and the land around it. Sally suspected her husband of more deviltry and told Tom to follow him at a distance to see what his father was up to. When Tom saw his father turn from the road to Listowel, and head for the Cowper Estate, he knew trouble would follow.

A few miles into the Cowper lands, Paddy found a new cottage with a barn alongside it. Tom stayed far enough away that his father couldn't see him. Dorset was tending sheep in a pasture, helped by a laborer walking beside him. No other cottages stood near, an ideal place for Paddy to snatch back Siobhan. The caravan could never cross the dense pastures, so he would have to grab her on horseback. About the baby he didn't care.

Some half a mile away, Tom observed the scene and raced back to his mother: "Mam, Da has found the cottage where Siobhan lives."

Unsurprised by the news, Sally made plans of her own. When Paddy went to the Harp and Shamrock in town, she left Tom in charge of the little ones and walked to St. Michael's. She knocked on the back door and met Sister Clare who was in the kitchen making supper. "Sister, I'm Sally O'Connor, Siobhan's mother. I know you've helped her a great deal, and I've come for your advice."

"Well," said Sister Clare, "Let's sit and have some tea."

While drinking their tea, Sally told the nun her worries: "I'm afraid that my husband, the devil, wants to capture Siobhan and return her as a traveler. He's been scouting her cottage. At least twice he's been nosing around her farm."

That evening Jeremy asked Siobhan, " Are you afraid of your father?"

"No," she said. "You and I are bound together forever. My father can't change that."

Sister Clare told Sean Kavanagh about the threat from O'Connor. Sean would alert the sheriff and the local farmers to be on the lookout for him. Sean asked if he should inform Jeremy and Siobhan to be on their guard, "Sure they've lived in peace over a year and been to Mass every Sunday with their baby." Sister Clare and Father Malloy both agreed that Sean should warn to the Dorsets, a task for which he was not anxious.

O'Connor

Paddy O'Connor scarcely mourned the death of his youngest daughter Eileen, so intent was he in recapturing his eldest, Siobhan, whom he could always sell for sex to keep him in drink. O'Connor thought moving the caravan from Listowel would lull his daughter and her husband into a false sense of security from his attempt to return her to the band. Three days after the burial of Eileen, O'Connor did the unusual and abstained from poitin all day, leading Sally to suspect his motives.

That night riding his best horse, O'Connor left the caravan headed for the Dorset cottage. Sally woke her son Tom and gave him the same instructions as before—to follow his father at a distance to see where he would go.

When O'Connor left the Listowel Road and bypassed the town, he knew where his father was headed—to the Dorset cottage. Tom raced back to tell his mother.

Guided by a full moon turning all the fields phosphorescent O'Connor rode through the Cowper Estate and arrived at the bottom of the hill below Jeremy and Siobhan's cottage when two watchdogs began to bark, and then charged the intruder. The dogs surprised O'Connor because they hadn't been there on his first trip. Forced to dismount because his horse became frightened, O'Connor suffered tears on his legs as the dogs tore into him.

"Goddamn curs," O'Connor swore.

Then the cottage door opened, and Siobhan burst out shotgun in hand with Jeremy limping behind her.

"Don't shoot," O'Connor yelled. "It's me, your father."

"You're no father to me," Siobhan yelled back.

Siobhan fired one barrel of the gun, aiming high to avoid hitting the dogs.

The shotgun pellets crashed into O'Connor's right shoulder, spinning him around, the dogs still hanging onto his legs.

"You bitch. You've shot me, my own daughter," Paddy yelled.

"We told you to stay away. Next time I'll kill you. Leave us in peace," Siobhan said.

Bleeding in the neck and shoulder, Paddy shook off the two dogs long enough to mount his horse and flee across the fields towards home.

The ride back to the caravan tortured O'Connor; his shoulder and neck still bleeding and sore from the gunshot, he struggled to rein in his horse. Sally met him as soon as he arrived. "Me own daughter shot me," O'Connor said.

"Did you hurt Siobhan, Jeremy, or the baby?" Sally asked.

"No, I couldn't get close to them."

"'Tis good enough for you," Sally said. "They warned you off."

"Woman, I need these pellets dug out of my shoulders and neck before they infect me."

"I won't do it. You have money for Drink. Go to go to a doctor who'll do it properly," Sally said.

"But in Listowel the sheriff will arrest me."

"Then go to Tralee and find a doctor who'll remove the shot," Sally said.

"Sure, that's seventeen miles, and I can't ride that far. You mean you won't do it?" O'Connor asked.

"No."

"When I'm healed, I'll give you a beating you'll never forget," O'Connor said.

"I haven't forgotten any of them."

Tom drove the caravan to Tralee with his father writhing in pain on a blanket in the back. In Tralee O'Connor found a doctor who dug out the buckshot, disinfected the wounds, and bandaged his shoulder and neck.

"Who shot you?" the doctor asked.

"That's my business," O'Connor said.

"You've lost much blood, recovery will be slow," the doctor said. "You must rest."

The caravan journeyed to Connemara, O'Connor's health improving each day. They encamped just outside Galway where O'Connor beat his wife for not tending his wounds, the children scattering to a tent in the woods to avoid the trouble. When Sally emerged from the caravan, she had two black eyes, which were beginning to look like a permanent feature of her face.

In Connemara O'Connor met the farmer, Jim Donnelly, from whom he would buy six ponies, the sale of which would keep him in poitín for weeks. Before they went to the pasture, Tom told his father, "You've drink taken. We'd best wait until tomorrow. This is dangerous work."

"Get away out of that," O'Connor said. "We'll catch the horses now."

One foal, a shiny brown with a white face, caught O'Connor's eye. He might even keep this one for himself. Disobeying his own rule about not working among a herd of horses milling about, O'Connor ignored the white stallion pawing nearby, looking to protect his offspring. As O'Connor lurched towards the foal, he stumbled trying to lasso him. The stallion charged, bucked, and with his hind feet kicked the man in the head, dropping him like a stone, the blood flowing freely from his head.

Chasing away the rest of the herd, Tom rushed over to his father and tried to shake him awake: "Da, Da," he said, "get up. The herd is moving around and may stomp on you." But his father would never hear him again.

Tom raced to the caravan, telling Sally what his happened. She ran with Tom to her husband to find him dead. What she had threatened to do for years, a Connemara pony had done for her.

Sally explained to Jim Donnelly what had happened, and he sold Tom the two ponies the boy had caught, and returned the rest of the money. Then Sally asked that they bury O'Connor in a corner of the field. He agreed, but warned them, "Bury him deep and don't tear up my pasture.'

Tom borrowed a shovel from Donnelly, and digging a deep trench buried his father.

Sally and Tom drove the caravan a few miles away into the woods, and the four of them emptied its contents: a black cauldron for cooking, some iron-forged tools, hand-made jewelry, candles, leatherwork, and woodwork. They then set fire to the van, a Traveler custom when the chief dies.

FOREBODINGS

Sister Clare walked to the market in Listowel one day and met a familiar face. Pale and thin, the man had lost an arm and had his left sleeve pinned to his shirt. "Jim Moran," she said. "I helped raise you at St. Michael's."

"Yes, Sister. You were kind to me. I've been too ashamed to come see you. People pity me and I hate it."

"What happened to you?"

"The American War," he said. "A minie ball destroyed my arm at the Battle of Antietam in Maryland. A doctor cut it off for fear of infection. A wonderful sister cleaned the wound saving my life."

"What is the war like?"

"Death and destruction, Sister. Other men lay dying and wounded on the field with no one to care for them. The only good thing was I sent my pay home to my family."

"What will you do now?"

"I won't beg, Sister."

"Jim, Sean Kavanaugh is always looking for laborers to do construction and farmers to tend sheep. So many have left to go to the war. His cottage is just down the road from St. Michael's. He might find work for you."

"Sister, God bless you."

When Jim talked with Sean Kavanagh who remembered him from St. Michael's, he said, "I'm sorry for your terrible injury, but with one good arm you can help building cottages and minding sheep. That will help you earn your keep. Come back tomorrow to start."

"Sean, I can't thank you enough."

The next day Jim started working with the group building the Dorset barn. He carried lumber and tools to the men. When Jeremy Dorset met Jim, he told the young man, "I'm planning to raise sheep and cows. Because of my disability, it's hard for me to get around. I could use a man to help me, and I'll pay you fairly."

"Thanks, Jeremy, that's a blessing to me."

When Sister Clare told Moran's story to Father Malloy, he said, "Our hierarchy has preached against young Irishmen joining the war. It's fine for them to say, but the war means work and money for our jobless. I do think many of our people will return to us maimed like Mike—those who aren't killed over there."

Jim's comment about the lack of nurses for the wounded touched Sister Clare. St. Michael's was now running smoothly after the worst of The Great Hunger. Her nursing skills could help the boys in the war. She would pray to the Lord for guidance about making the choice the Lord would want."

Sister Clare and Palmerston

One sunny afternoon while cantering on his big brown horse down Listowel Road, Palmerston met a tall woman dressed in religious garb coming out of St. Michael's. Normally mild-mannered, Sister Clare chastised Palmerston, "Out looking for more girls to ravish? Why can you not restrain your desires like other Christian men?"

"You're one of those Catholic nuns hiding away in a convent muttering Latin prayers to a Papist God. How dare you impugn my morals when you closet yourself away from all men. Probably a lesbian. Are you afraid of men?" asked Palmerston.

"No," the nun retorted, "I'm around children and men all day."

Just then Sean Kavanagh came riding up on his way to Listowel and heard some of Palmerston's invective. "Palmerston," Sean said, "have you stooped so low as to criticize a religious woman who serves the poor?"

"She's nothing but a Papist bitch," Pamerston yelled. "And she railed at me first. Some day we'll be rid of you all with your rosaries and superstitions."

"Palmerston, you better be off with your evil mouth," Sean said.

"One day you'll all pay," Palmerston said.

Sean said, "I don't know when or how, but some day it's you who will pay."

When the man had ridden away, Sean said, "Sister, pay him no mind. He's a bad man. You know we all love you."

"God bless you, Sean," said Sister Clare. "I pray for that man, but my prayers haven't reached heaven."

"As you taught us, Sister, prayer is never wasted."

A New Life

After O'Connor's death, one of the other bands of travelers asked if Sally and her family wished to join them. Sally declined because she and the children would still be travelers begging for food and living on the road. Instead Sally traded the two ponies and some money for a caravan. After four days they reached Listowel, St. Michael's and Sister Clare. The first thing the nun did was feed them. Sally sent the kids outside to play while she spoke to the nun: "Sister, my husband is dead, kicked in the head by a horse in Connemara. I want my children and me to give up the traveler life and get an education, the two little ones, Caitlin six and Mavourneen eight. Could I enroll them here at St. Michael's?"

"Of course," said Sister Clare. "It will be a change for them at first, but the young can adapt. I'll speak to Father Malloy, but it won't be a problem."

Sally continued, "My son Tom, thirteen, is my biggest worry because my husband's evil infected him for the longest time. Could we give him a trial here, like?"

"Yes, I'll take him under my wing and give him a good opportunity," Sister Clare said. "Also, Sean Kavanagh has an empty house near him, the one Jeremy and Siobhan lived in before they built their farm. It would be a short walk to school for the children."

Sally hugged the nun.

Sally told the children what she had decided, the girls excited about the prospect of school, Tom more reticent: "Mam, I'll be way behind the other boys"

"Tom, if we are settled people, you'll have to get an education."

Sister Clare accompanied the little group to the Kavanagh's where Sean and Mary welcomed them, Sally's daughters thrilled to make new friends with the Kavanagh children. Sean helped Sally and Tom unload the caravan at their new home. Sean said, "Jeremy and Siobhan live four miles north over those small hills. You'll have to walk there because the fields are too thick for the van."

At the end of their walk, the little girls scurried to the cottage to see Siobhan and the baby, the dogs not bothering them. When Siobhan saw them, she was afraid at first that her father had returned. When Sally came into the house, she said, "Your father is dead, buried in a field in Connemara."

Siobhan cried, a mixture of sadness and relief, saying, "Mam, I'm sorry he's gone, but he'll never threaten us again."

"Yes," Sally said.

The girls dove on the floor to see the baby crawl. Seeing baby Sally, her grandmother cried. She told Siobhan that she had enrolled the children at St. Michael's; they would be settled people, on the road no more.

JUSTICE

Recovered from his wounds, Palmerston wanted to hurt Dorset for abandoning him and marrying. He would take the tinker girl as he had in the field weeks ago. When he was ready, he scouted the Dorset cottage from a distance and saw no problems except for some watchdogs. He had no fear of Jeremy. He wrapped some meat in a canvas sack to distract the dogs before he went after Siobhan.

Palmerston rode up as close as he dared to the cottage. When the dogs challenged him, he threw the meat on the ground. The barking dogs alerted Jeremy and Siobhan to trouble. Hobbling up to the door, Palmerston discovered it locked, so he pounded on it. "Jeremy," he yelled," it's me. Open up. We have some business to conduct."

Jeremy yanked the door open quickly, so that Palmerston fell face forward on the floor, Jeremy standing over him with a shotgun. "Don't shoot, it's me," Palmerston said. Siobhan was in the kitchen holding the baby.

Jeremy fired one barrel just over Palmerston's head, saying, "The next barrel will be in your chest."

Surprised by Jeremy's anger, Palmerston scrambled outside for his horse, but he couldn't leave without a threat. He yelled, "I'll be back again, when you least expect, and I'll enjoy your tinker wife again. She'll have a real man to satisfy her."

Infuriated by Palmerston's threats, Jeremy gave chase to the devil, asking Siobhan to hand him the gun, "No, Jeremy, I don't want to lose you to a murder charge."

Even though Palmerston had a head start, Jeremy took a shortcut, saving ground and forcing his enemy towards the Listowel Road, where an open gate for cows loomed ahead. Jeremy was just behind Palmerston when he whacked the man's horse on the rump with his riding crop.

Startled, Palmerston's horse bucked, catapulting its rider from his saddle head over heels against a wall of flat stones lining the road. The blow crushed Palmerston's skull, leaking gray brain matter and blood. Coming up the road, Sean Kavanagh saw the whole scene unfold. He told Dorset, "I'll ride for the sheriff."

When Sheriff Costello arrived, he asked Dorset and Sean what had happened. Sean said, "A red fox darted across the road spooking Palmerston's horse." Dorset said the same.

The sheriff said, "Don't touch a thing. I'll get the coroner and Captain Davison to verify the cause of death. The man was a beast, but his father is important in England, so I'll have to write a thorough report. I'll cordon off the road."

When Lord Palmerston read the dragoon's account of his son's death, he sent money to ship the body back to Sheffield to lie with his ancestors at the family estate. "I don't want him buried among you papists," he wrote to Sheriff Costello. Right now I'm very busy negotiating with the Confederacy to act on their side in the Civil War."

Jeremy arrived home trembling. "Siobhan, I caused an accident that killed Palmerston. I didn't tell the sheriff the full account, and neither did Sean Kavanagh who saw it all happen."

Siobhan said, "It's good enough for him. Palmerston was evil, come here to rape me. Don't say a word more."

"Yes, love," Jeremy said.

"I know you feel bad about the devil's death, but he got the end he deserved."

That afternoon when Sean Kavanagh told Mary the full details of Palmerton's death, that Jeremy had whipped the horse and said nothing about it, Mary said, "Good. Keep quiet about it. The monster has caused enough trouble. One thing you might do is ride over to Jeremy and assure him you'll say no more."

Sean rode to Jeremy and Siobhan's. He said to them both: "It was an accident. You didn't mean to kill the man. Don't blame yourself. I'll keep my peace."

Siobhan said, "The devil came to rape me, Jeremy fired a shot over his head to scare him off and then pursued him when the accident happened."

Sean said, "He died the way he lived, trying to fulfill his lust. Farmers will no longer have to fear for their daughters out working in the fields or walking the roads alone. Worry about him no more. We're well rid of him"

DOMESTIC BLISS

Jeremy and Siobhan were overjoyed. "I'm pregnant again, Mam, and we're happy."

Jeremy said, "We'll build you a house next to ours after the harvest."

Sally said, "You're a good, good man. Bless the day Siobhan married you."

While the children attended school, Sally earned some money working at Josie's knitting shop in town. Now that Siobhan had learned to read, she tutored her sisters.

One day when Sally and Siobhan were home minding the baby, Sally asked "Mam, why was Da so evil?"

"God knows. Part of it was The Drink, the curse of all traveling men. He knew no life apart from being a traveler. He treated us the way he himself was treated. I loved him when we were young, but he ended up making me hate him. Look how he treated you, his own flesh and blood."

Embracing her mother, Siobhan said. "Mam, you held us together all those years".

After Sally O'Connor became a settled person, she needed money. St. Michael's fed and schooled her children, but she wanted to earn her own way. Josie Mullins, now married to Frank Collins, asked Sally to assist her in her knitting shop in Listowel. From Josie, Sally learned the prices of the woolen sweaters and scarves they sold, including those that Siobhan made under her tutelage from Sister Clare.

Sister Clare and the Mullins' sisters gave Sally and her children clothes that transformed them from travelers into residents of Listowel. The girls were doing fine at St. Michael's learning to read and write, and Tom had progressed also, no longer afraid of being backward with the older boys in school. He had lost all desire of being on the road

At the shop the most difficult task Sally had to learn was how to treat customers. But the most important change was in Sally because Josie taught her a new sense of self-respect. Josie helped Sally make herself an equal to those from whom she had once begged food.

Josie showed her how to stand firm with customers who demanded lower prices than the knits were worth. One day a local farmer, Dan Ryan, came into the store and chose a heavy green sweater. "I'll pay no more than one pound for this," Ryan said.

"Then you'd better take your business elsewhere, Sir. That sweater took days to make."

Ryan said, "A pound and a half then."

Josie replied, "The price is two pounds, Sir, and worth every bit of it. Try it on."

After Ryan put on the sweater, he asked Josie and Sally, "How does it fit?"

Josie said "It's a large, just your build. I'll even add a matching scarf at no extra cost."

The sweater and scarf pleased the man and he paid the two pounds.

Sally had watched the entire transaction and said, "Josie, you're very good at this." Josie said, "You can learn to do it. You're smart and have a good sense of people. Forget about your past. You're one of us now. Also, I'm pregnant and going to have a baby soon, so I'll need you to manage the shop."

Sally was ready to cry, but a new customer came into the shop; and Sally made her wait on the lady, the sale coming off without a hitch. Overjoyed, Sally joined Sister Clare's knitting class to learn more about her craft.

At harvest time, Jeremy Dorset came into the shop telling Sally he had workers to build her family their own cottage not far from his own. "Jeremy, sure I'm embarrassed that I don't have the money to pay you."

"Sally, you and the children are family. My farm is thriving. We have enough money to pay for your cottage and a small farm. If it makes you feel better, we'll consider it a loan. Pay it back when you can."

Sally wept at Jeremy's generosity: "You're the kindest man I've ever known."

Jeremy said, "You've given me Siobhan whose value to me is far beyond money."

In late summer Jeremy hired and supervised the same laborers who had built his own cottage—including Jim Moran who had adapted to his injury. The men were glad for the work. Sean Kavanagh, Joseph, and young Tom helped when they could. When the workers finished the cottage, Sally cried with joy, saying to Siobhan and Jeremy, "I'm so thankful to you both. I've almost forgotten all those terrible years."

"Mam, you deserve it, keeping us a family all that time." To her mother, Siobhan said, "I'm pregnant, and soon you'll have another grandchild."

Sister Clare came to the Kavanaghs one afternoon and said to Sean and Mary, "I've received a letter from our Mother General that the Moore family is living in Dublin and having difficulties. They've no money, and their three little ones are living in an orphanage close by. Is there any way we can get them a cottage and maybe a farm near here? I hate to ask you to take on more work."

"Sister, you know that we love you and will do anything you ask. The Moores were a victim of Palmerston's tumbling. We haven't forgotten them. As it happens we have an empty cottage now that Sally and her family have moved near the Dorsets. In time we can build them their own place."

"Sean, that would be wonderful."

"Michael Moore is an excellent farmer, and he could help out both Jeremy and me until he can get on his feet and carve out his own farm. I'll speak to Jeremy and see if he has any land for them."

"Sean, you're a Godsend," Sister Care said.

"I'll have to speak to Mary if she minds me being gone for two days. I can borrow Dick Peters' big wagon to bring the Moores back here."

"God bless you, Sean, "Sister Clare said. "I'll give you precise direction to Baggot Street, our motherhouse where the Moores are staying. The orphanage with the Moore children is nearby."

When Father Malloy heard the news, he gave Sean five pounds for food on the journey. "Sean," he said, "this is one more act of kindness you're doing."

"Thanks, Father, but it will be good to help the Moores after the tumbling."

When Sean told Mary about the trip, she said, "Let me give you some blankets for the ride. Sister Clare and Josie will give you some clothes for them."

Borrowing the Peters' wagon, Sean left home early the next morning. He had to travel through Limerick, Abberlieux, and Naas to reach the city. When Sean picked up the Moores at Baggot Street and the little ones at the orphanage, the family was overjoyed.

After they reached home, Sean settled them in the cottage. Jeremy Dorset rode by and said, "I've got some land for them, but it needs clearing and much hard work."

Sean said, "Michael Moore doesn't mind hard work, but he'll have to borrow some tools from you until he can buy his own."

"Fine," Jeremy said. "I can use some help myself."

Sean told Moore about the land, and he was excited to start. "No more tumblings," Sean said. "Jeremy owns the land."

Moore told Sean, "I'll be thankful to you until the day I die. You've saved my family."

A New Project

Many veterans began to drift home from America. And then Sister Clare received a jolt when her youngest brother Denis wrote her from his home in Dundalk:

> "Dear Sis,
>
> I've decided to enlist in the war and join the Irish Brigade in New York. I do not know how I'll fare, but our brothers and sisters will manage the farm and take care of Ma and Da, especially Joan. I know you will worry about me.
>
> One request: Pray for me hard.
>
> Your loving brother, Denis."

At least the veterans had their American pensions. Many of the Irish Brigade were still in shock, wearing their service on their faces. Some men came home to find their wives had died, their homes empty. Sister Clare hit on the idea of establishing a home for soldiers, some to recuperate and move on, the maimed in need of care. Sister Clare went to Father Malloy and told him of her idea. The priest said, " Now you're finding more work for yourself, but I've learned that nothing stands in your way. I'll donate land from my pasture and give you some money from church. I'll help in any way I can."

Next, Sister Clare went to Sean Kavanagh. "Would you help me build a house for soldiers returning from the war?"

"Sister," he said, "I can deny you nothing. I can get free labor from the farmers after the harvest. Jeremy Dorset will donate money for wood and supplies."

"The house must have many individual rooms for these men to have some privacy," Sister Clare said.

"That's easily done."

That fall, building commenced. Sister Clare envisioned a place where she could provide some nursing care for the disabled. With her experience from hospitals in Dublin, she knew what she wanted. The physically fit could find work on the farms since so many thers had left. She would call the place "St. Michael's Rest Home for Soldiers." She would live at the house to be close to the men. The building was ready in the fall with room for twelve soldiers. Jeremy and Siobhan Dorset donated beds, and several farmers, skilled carpenters, made a kitchen table with chairs.

Her first resident was Joe Condon from the Irish Brigade who was without a home. He told Sister Clare "I fought at Fredericksburg and Gettysburg. Then my time was up."

Jim Moran, the one-armed soldier who had learned to work even with his disability, asked Sister Clare "May I live at the home?' Me wife has died leaving me no other family"

"Of course," said the nun, "that's why it's here."

For those veterans still recovering from their wounds, Sister Clare enlisted Doctor Driscoll in town for his aid. Each resident had his own room with a bed and took their meals in a common room, the food cooked by Sister Clare at nearby St. Michael's and carried over to the home by the school children. Some of the men had visitors, relatives or friends, a practice Sister Clare encouraged to lift her patients' morale.

THE AMERICAN CIVIL WAR AND IRELAND

The regimental flag of the "Fighting 69th" New York Infantry –
Used by the Irish Brigade throughout the Civil War

Eleven years after the end of The Great Hunger, Civil War erupted in America. The war spurred much interest in Ireland. Northern recruiters combed the country and promised jobless Irishmen, especially those with no land, free passage to America, a bounty from $100 to $700, American citizenship, and the chance to buy cheap farmland. The opportunity to flee from British landlordism enticed 140,000 young Irish to fight in this war, most of them for the North—even though the Catholic hierarchy preached against it.

American newspapers like The *New York Irish American* called the Irish to arms "because of the sacred memories of the past, by your remembrance of the succor extended to your suffering brethren, by the future hope of your native land here taking root . . . to be true to the land of your adoption in this crisis. The *Boston Pilot* was even more direct: "Stand by the Union;

fight for the Union; die by the Union (The Society of the Irish Brigade home.earthlink.net)"

Two Irish men, O'Malley and Prendergast, dressed in Union blue and carrying the flag of the Irish Brigade, rode into Listowel and visited farms in the area to make their pitch for recruits. Many young men felt a loyalty to the nation that had been a sanctuary for their people during and after The Great Hunger.

Some Irish patriots saw the war as an opportunity to acquire military skills in hopes of waging war against England as Fenians (from the Irish word "Finn", an archaic term meaning "warrior") But their efforts later failed in an attack against Canada, a British colony, in the Battle of Ridgeway, and still later in 1867 against the English at Chester Castle in Ireland.

Over 140,000 Irish joined the American Civil War with lofty expectations, unaware of the savage combat that lay in wait for them.

Though tempted by the chance to buy cheap farmland in America and escape the tyranny of England, Sean Kavanagh, now in his early forties, was too old for such an adventure as the American war. He had a family to support, and he had to cultivate his farm. Besides he had had his fill of violence after escaping from the dragoons years before.

> "The American war touches Ireland more deeply than almost any other country in the world. For every parish in Ireland, there is at the other side of the Atlantic an almost corresponding colony of people, bound by ties of affection and blood. In their sufferings our own people suffer."
>
> Cork Examiner, June, 10, 1861.

According to Fox's *Regimental Losses* "of all Union Army brigades, only the Vermont Brigade and the Iron Brigade suffered more combat dead than the Irish." After the first day of fighting at Fredericksburg, the Irish Brigade lost 545 men, 45 percent of the men it took into battle.

At least 4000 Irish died in the fighting. The Irish Brigade fought valiantly at Fredericksburg, Gettysburg, the Wilderness, Spotsylvania, and in other battles.

In addition to soldiers over 600 Irish women, from eight different orders volunteered to serve as nurses during the war, chiefly the Sisters of Mercy and Mother Seton's Sisters of Charity. The work of the nuns was heroic. Mary Livermore future women's rights leader who worked with the U.S. Sanitary Commission, said: "I am neither a Catholic, nor an advocate of the monastic institutions of that church . . . But I can never forget my experience during the War of the Rebellion . . . Never did I meet these Catholic sisters in hospitals, on transports, or hospital steamers, without observing their devotion, faithfulness, and unobtrusiveness. They gave themselves no airs of superiority or holiness, shirked no duty, sought no easy place, bred no mischiefs. Sick and wounded men watched for their entrance into the wards at morning, and looked a regretful farewell when they departed at night (*CHAUSA* | *Sisters of Charity of Cincinnati*.)" Members of these religious orders went back to Ireland to recruit more members.

"Irish immigrants" *(Irish American_wikipedia).*

ENGLAND AND THE CIVIL WAR

"The Ignorant Vote-Honors are Easy," by Thomas Nast
cartoons.osu.edu/nast/ignorant vote.htm

Irish presence in the war warned England of the consequences in
Ireland should Britain intervene because many of the Union Irish soldiers
were revolutionaries who would turn against. Britain.

Always interested in furthering its own agenda, Mother England kept
a watchful eye on the American war. The Confederacy was the world's
largest producer of cotton intended for mills in England and France—
making foreign intervention on its behalf a possibility. To run the Union
blockade of cotton ships, the English even built three ships for the South,
the most famous of which was the CSS *Alabama* sunk by the Union ship
Kearsage outside Cherbourg in 1862.

Britain conducted secret negotiations with the South which came
to light with the *Trent* affair in 1861 when an American ship *San Jacinto*
captured two Confederate emissaries, Mason and Slidell, aboard the

English ship Trent with documents asking for English aid. The incident sparked controversy in both England and America, but Washington apologized for the affair and returned the two ambassadors to the South, ending the dispute.

With Lincoln's Emancipation Proclamation, Jan. 1 1863, he made it difficult for nations that had abolished slavery to support the South. English philosopher John Stewart Mills wrote, "The triumph of the Confederacy would be a victory for the powers of evil which would give courage to the enemies of progress." The Proclamation meant that foreign powers in favor of the South would be supporting a nation whose economy was based on a racist institution that these nations had abandoned years before. In "Turning the Tide, "from *The US News and World Report,* Curry writes, "With a stroke [of his pen], Lincoln had eliminated the international question." The defeat at Gettysburg dashed any hope for foreign intervention for the Confederacy.

A Good Death

For the families of Irish soldiers in the American Civil War, the possibility that their loved ones might not have a 'good death,' a Catholic death attended to by a priest was a constant fear. In a society accustomed to experiencing death by their family's bedsides, the remoteness of many Civil War fatalities denied family members the opportunity to witness their relation's all-important final moments. An awareness of this 'need to know' led to efforts by many companions and care-givers to inform families of a soldier's preparedness to meet His maker, if and when the time came. The mother of Irishman Captain Hugh McQuade received just such a letter from Richmond in 1861, as her son, wounded at Bull Run, fought to recover from the amputation of his leg. He had been wounded and captured during First Bull Run on 21st July 1861. The severity of his wound necessitated the removal of his lower left leg. Sister Valentine, one of the Catholic Sisters of Charity caring for the wounded in Richmond, felt the time appropriate to write to Hugh's mother outlining his situation, assuring her of his stoicism and that he had made his peace with God.

From General Hospital No. 1 in Richmond where Sister Valentine wrote to Hugh McQuade's mother (original letter in Library of Congress).

> "You may sometimes imagine that your son is in need of something; but permit me to assure you, dear madam, that he is surrounded with every care that a mother's affection could devise, or a mother's hands bestow. We only desire to be able to make him more comfortable; we have procured for him a nice little private room, which removes him from every annoyance, and promotes that quiet his state so much requires.
>
> That he is truly happy, there is no doubt. He intends

preparing himself for the amputation by a devout reception of the sacraments, so that in case he is called he will be prepared. What a great satisfaction for you. What greater happiness or higher hope can a Christian mother claim than to see her child submitting himself, willing and loving, to the disposal of his Creator. But you will pray for him as a mother only can pray. Beg for him the prayers of the poor and the orphans, for their prayers pierce the Heavens and reach the ear of God. Uniting myself to your prayers, I remain,

Most Respectfully Yours,
Sister Valentine"

Hugh McQuade died in Richmond as a result of his wounds on 26th December, 1861.

This letter was reprinted in Irish newspapers and stirred Sister Clare. She wrote to the War Department in Washington for the names and addresses of Irish killed in battle because she would write their families to give them some comfort. This was an immense task, but she would enlist her friends to help. Two months later a reply came. Sadly, many men were missing in action, 4000 killed or wounded in the Battle of Fredericksburg alone. Sister Clare received consolation from the fact that 580 nuns served as nurses in the Civil War, may of them Irish coming from the Sisters of Mercy and the Sisters of Charity.

THE KAVANAGHS

Sean and Mary Kavanagh with their children and grandchildren survived the end of the Great Hunger, English landlordism, and tyrants like Palmerston. The Dorsets found peace after escaping the Travelers. Sister Clare would continue to run St. Michael's and her rest home for Civil War veterans. As for the Quakers, they petitioned Parliament for land reform in Ireland.

In the end all were survivors.

THE DEAD KEEP ON DYING

Evidence of famine horrors continues such as the monument to the Irish in Montreal.
The Irish Stone: Montreal
(Photo: Krikor Tersakian)

> "To preserve from desecration the remains of 6000 immigrants who died of ship
> fever A.D. 1847-48. This stone is erected by the workmen of Messrs. Peto, Brassey
> and Betts employed in the construction of the Victoria Bridge A.D. 1859"
> The Irish Stone: Montreal

A pier of the Victoria Bridge (1853-59) was built on a graveyard for
Famine victims who had died in Montreal. These survivors from coffin ships
were re-interred at this location memorialized by the largest boulder retrieved
from the St. Lawrence River by truck during construction. The builders hired
an artist to inscribe the stone, probably the oldest Famine memorial in the
world. It is also a testament to the Irish workers who constructed the bridge
from 1853-1859. The laborers showed a national sensibility and kindness
rarely seen elsewhere irish-genealogy-toolkit.com/coffin-ships.html).

More Dead

A more recent discovery of the tragedy of The Great Hunger occurred in 2005 at a building site in Kilkenny. According to Dare Kelly, a staff writer for IrishCentral.com, the excavation of a Victorian workhouse revealed the remains of almost 1,000 famine victims. The majority of the bodies found were infants and children.

"The most startling discovery was that there were so many children among the dead, particularly children aged two through six," osteoarchaeological scientist, Jonny Geber, told the Irish Times.

Social research has ignored the deaths of children in The Great Hunger when millions died because there were few records. The worst disease afflicting the children was scurvy because of the lack of vitamin C, which the potato had provided. "This is unique. This burial ground was completely unknown, it had been lost in local memory," Geber says.

The dead passed away between 1845 and 1852 and were buried in deep pits, containing between 6 and 27 people. All were interred in coffins and stacked on top of each other. ("One thousand famine victims found in Irish burial site." *Irish Central News* Dublin. 21 Oct. 2011 Print.

Aftermath

The Journal of Economic History points out the draining of Ireland's population at the conclusion of the Great Hunger:

> After The Great Hunger, emigration from Ireland was roughly five times the number who died in the Famine. According to the *Journal of Economic History,"* poverty and low wages, large family size, and limited opportunities to acquire smallholdings contributed to the high rate of emigration."

Young farmers abandoned Ireland because they couldn't buy smallholdings, resulting in joblessness. This mass emigration was five times larger than the million who had died in The Great Hunger, more than double that of any other European country (*"Journal of Economic History,"* 1993, Hatton and Williamson.

After the famine, inexpensive Indian corn became the chief source of sustenance for the poor. Because the maize had to be milled twice, the Irish didn't take to it very well, but they used it to feed pigs and poultry making meat and eggs more available. Farmers later turned to homegrown oatmeal. By 1867 the Irish diet consisted of potatoes, whole meal bread, and porridge from oatmeal. Turnips and cabbage also became staples of Irish food. "While there were still many Irish who were poor, the population could at least eat." And the system of land ownership changed. Instead of breaking up farms into smaller units, the holding was conferred upon the eldest son, and the other sons moved to the cities or emigrated (History of Irish Food—Do Chara").

In 1879 a second potato blight occurred, chiefly in the west of Ireland, but the Irish were now more prepared. Charles Stewart Parnell founded the Land League, politically organizing farmers and lobbying England for land reform.

"The Wyndham Act of 1913 allowed most Irish tenants to purchase their holdings from their landlords with British government assistance." (The History Place—Irish Potato Famine)"

"In 1949 seven hundred years of British rule in Ireland was ended as The Republic of Ireland was finally proclaimed. . . "(The History Place—Irish Potato Famine/After).

Irish Food for English Stomachs

In the aftermath of the Famine, Kinealy points out the draining of Ireland's population: "the numbers leaving Ireland showed no signs of abating until the 1850s, and continued to be an integral part of the Irish lifecycle in the second half of the nineteenth century. Not surprisingly, emigration acquired the properties of a paradox. Leaving Ireland simultaneously represented both escape and exile. As the century progressed, a culture of exile emerged, reinforced by a whole system of leave taking, which included American 'wakes,' a bottle night and supper, a farewell procession of friends and neighbors and a final blessing from a local priest."

Kinealy, *This Great Calamity* (303

"As a proportion of the population, the rate of emigration from Ireland was more than double that of any other European country. The Irish population fell from 6.5 million to 4.4 million between 1851 and 1916." After the Famine, "Arrest, remand, do anything you can," counseled Charles Wood, Chancellor of the Exchequer, to Lord Clarendon, the ranking British official in Ireland. "Rate collectors seized livestock, furniture or anything else of value . . . had been extracted from the Irish. . . ." (History Place) What did the poor Irish farmers have left? They had lost their homes, their furnishings and their livestock. No wonder that 150,000 Irish joined the Civil War in America where they had at least acquired money, a pension, American citizenship, and a chance to buy farmland free from the oppressor's yoke.

The second failure of the potato crop in 1846 left many people without access to their usual supply of food. The Whig government's decision not to intervene in the market place but to use public works as the main means of providing relief was disastrous. In many instances, the wages paid on the relief works proved to be too low to purchase food in a period of 'famine' prices,' causing hoarding. At the same time, large amounts of food continued to leave Ireland and it was not until the following spring that food imports became substantial. Consequently, during the winter, there was a 'starvation gap'. The size of that gap is best measured, not in calorific values or in terms of the volume of food exported, but in the amount of excess mortality and suffering during those months. Whilst official mortality statistics were not kept, the local Irish constabulary provided an unofficial estimate that 400,000 people had died due to a lack of food.

Kinealy, Christine. *The Great Irish Famine* 1845-1850 nde.state

Kinealy states that almost 4,000 vessels carried food from Ireland to the ports of Bristol, Glasgow, Liverpool and London during 1847, when 400,000 Irish men, women and children died of starvation and related diseases. The food was shipped under guard from the most famine-stricken parts of Ireland: Ballina, Ballyshannon, Bantry, Dingle, Killala, Kilrush, Limerick, Sligo, Tralee and Westport. *The Great Irish Famine* 1845-1850 (nde.state). 12 Dec. 2012.

Modern Day Controversy and Hope

Today's Irish scholars of The Great Hunger have divided themselves into two camps, the traditionalists and the revisionists. In her book *The Great Calamity* Christine Kinealy has summarized the two positions:

> "Recent scholarly studies of the Famine have moved away from this traditional view [that greedy English landlords caused the distress in Ireland]. In doing so a sanitized alternative has emerged that has endeavored to remove the patina of blame from the authorities involved in providing relief while minimizing the suffering of those most directly affected by the loss of the potato, reducing the overall population of the country but also of strengthening and increasing the influence of the class to which they (English aristocrats) belonged." (342). "The strand of thinking . . . commenced in the 1960s with Raymond Crotty . . . and in the 1990s with Roy Foster. Some of these conclusions have recently been challenged by Joel Mokyr, James Donnelly Jnr and Cormac O'Grada, amongst others."
>
> (xvi).

Duggan points out the revisionist views of E. R. R.Green in his book *The Course of Irish History* "we need to be clear in our minds that this (the Famine) was primarily a disaster like a flood or earthquake. The blight was natural, no one can be held responsible for that. Conditions in Ireland which had placed thousands and thousands of people in dependence on the potato are another matter. Yet the historian, if he is conscientious, will have an uneasy conscience about labeling any class or individuals as villains of the piece." The Irish have no such scruples in laying the blame for the Great Hunger on England's doorstep.

Kinealy points out that The Great Hunger presented Britain with the opportunity to control the dangers of a Catholic neighbor and to effect a restructuring of Ireland's land and agricultural economy for its own benefit.

England carried out this same philosophy in Scotland also, the "Highland Clearances," which forced thousands of Scots to emigrate as well. (3)

Tim Pat Coogan also challenges the revisionists: "there are those who would still attempt to defend the Whig's role on the grounds that the Geneva Convention on Genocide stems from 1948, not 1848. To them I say there is an even older command on which the declaration draws, and it is not disputed—"Thou shalt not kill." Coogan, *The Famine Plot* (2)

Former Prime Minister Tony Blair's apology for the Famine has helped stop the spread of Revisionism: he writes the Famine was a defining moment in the history of Ireland and Britain. It has left deep scars. That one million people should have died in what was then part of then part of the richest and most powerful nations of the world is something that still causes pain as we reflect on it today. Those who governed in England at the time failed the people." Quoted by Coogan (7-8}.

GENOCIDE

> "'Genocide' is a legal term with a precise definition that has been determined by the 1948 Geneva Convention." What follows are acts of genocide:
> a. Killing members of the group;
> b. Causing serious bodily or mental harm to members of the group;
> c. Deliberately inflicting on the group conditions of life calculated to bring about its physical destruction in whole or in part;
> d. Imposing measures to prevent births within the group;
> e. Forcibly transferring children of that group to another group. . . ."
> . . . during the years 1845-1850 the British government knowingly pursued a policy of mass starvation in Ireland that constituted acts of genocide against the Irish People within the meaning of Article II (b) and Article II (c) of the 1948 Geneva Convention."
>
> *("The Famine Was Genocide")*

Professor of International Law at the University of Illinois, Francis Boyle makes an irrefutable legal argument for the Famine as genocide:

In 1996, Boyle wrote a report commissioned by the New York-based Irish Famine/Genocide Committee, which concluded that the British government deliberately pursued a race and ethnicity-based policy aimed at destroying the group commonly known as the Irish people and that the policy of mass starvation amounted to genocide per the Hague convention of 1948. On the strength of Boyle's report, the U.S. state of New Jersey included the famine in the "Holocaust and Genocide Curriculum" at the secondary tier. Other states like New York have adopted the history of The Great Hunger as part of their curriculum. Boyle remarks further: "Clearly, during the years 1845-1850, the British government pursued a policy of mass starvation in Ireland with intent to destroy in substantial part the national, ethnical, and racial group commonly known as the Irish people as such. In addition this British policy of mass starvation in Ireland clearly caused serious bodily and mental harm to members of the Irish people within the meaning of the genocide Convention Article II (b)."

Britain's failure to prevent starvation in Ireland was genocide. England had her own people on the ground in Ireland telling her how bad things were-- the head of the Poor Law Edward Twistleton, the Irish aristocrat Lord Monteagle, writer Asenath Nicholson, Lord Clarendon, and the Quakers who spoke to Parliament while Britain still exported food from a starving country. "There is some truth, then, in John Mitchel's claim that in the 1840s 'Ireland died of political economy'." Quoted in *Atlas (652)*. As proof of this British parsimony toward Ireland in a time of crisis is the fact that the British spent about 7 millions pounds, less than one half of one percent of the gross nation product for those years. (The History Place). Also, as David Randall points out in his article in the Independent " Britain's colonial shame: Slave-owners given huge payouts after . . . the abolition of slavery," England paid 21 million pounds to Barbados in reparation for slavery, three times what it spent on Irish relief after the Famine. One British newspaper put the matter succinctly that there is only one book the English believe in, the ledger. John Mitchel claims that in the 1840s 'Ireland died of political economy'." Quoted in *Atlas (652)*.

WHY?

History Corner: The Great Irish Famine

S.J. Duggan explains that the English peasant class did not cause the Famine. English aristocrats saw the devastation as "God's way of thinning out the Papist tribes as being less than human." *Punch* cartoons of the time give ample illustration of this:

England and the Irish Monkey
Punch, XL (May 25, 1861):213

STEVE TAYLOR VIEWS OF THE FAMINE

THE BRITISH LION AND THE IRISH MONKEY.
Monkey (Mr. Mitchel). "One of us MUST be 'Put Down.'"

Monkey (John Mitchel). "One of us MUST be 'Put Down.'"

STEVE TAYLOR VIEWS OF THE FAMINE

An article in *Punch* 1862 satirizes the Irish immigrants: "A creature manifestly between the gorilla and the Negro is to be met in some of the lowest districts of London and Liverpool . . . It belongs in fact to a tribe of Irish savages." Quoted by Kinealy (331). This is racism pure and simple, reminiscent of the Nazi genocide of the Jews who were untermenschen (sub-human). Denying a race's humanity makes it much easier to destroy them. The Nazis used a system of mechanized genocide, the English starvation.

These cartoons reflect common English government's feeling toward the Irish. Modern scholar Tim Pat Coogan cites English historian James Anthony Froude: "the people in Catholic Ireland "were more like tribes of squalid apes than human beings." Thomas Carlyle wrote "Ireland is a starved rat that crosses the path of an elephant: what is the elephant to do? Squelch it, by heaven! Squelch it!" Quoted in "Official British Intent—Irish Holocaust" (1) And squelch it Britain did allowing the Irish "rat" to perish.

Coogan points out that a similar potato blight in Scotland, brought no catastrophic number of deaths, but in Ireland a different mentality ruled. The Irish would receive punishment from God for their Catholicism. After a visit to Ireland in a letter to the *Morning Post*, Sir Charles Trevelyan explained that at least a million had to die in Ireland: "Protestant and Catholic will freely fall and the land will be for the survivors." Quoted by Coogan (2).

Trevelyan publicly scolded British Coast Inspector Sir James Dombrain for giving free handouts of food to the starving. Dombrain answered "There was no one within many miles who could have contributed one shilling... The people were actually dying." (History Place). As his reason for denying food to the Irish, Trevelyan proclaimed, "The real evil with which we have to contend is not the physical evil of the Famine but the moral evil of the selfish, perverse and turbulent character of the people "multitext.ucc.ie/d/ Charles_Edward_Trevelyan..

Tim Pat Coogan in his blog *Plot* contends that today's Irish economy is "depending on doles from Brussels, the IMF and so on. And we're back to unemployment, emigration, and suicide—and of course, to learned helplessness." (Blog)

Coogan cites Earl Grey, the colonial secretary of Ireland in 1846: "We have a military occupation of Ireland, but in no other sense can it be said to be governed." Jimmy Breslin makes the same point—Ireland did not govern itself. England did. Coogan goes on to say what other historians have claimed—that the silence which came after The Great Hunger came from her fear of its powerful emotive and political force. Tim Pat Coogan. " This silence is summarized in an Irish aphorism, 'Whatever you say, say nothing.' Ni Dhomnaill asserts "It is our present total and almost willful amnesia about the hidden way of life that I see as the most lasting scar of the Great Famine." Hayden (68).

Coogan, Tim Pat "A policy of ethnic cleansing? Who's to blame for the Irish Famine?" IrishCentral.com. Interview with Cahir O'Doherty. 8 Dec. 2012. Web.

Kinealy explains another long-range consequence of The Great Hunger: "The descendants of those who fled to the United States from famine-stricken Ireland kept alive in the Irish-American community a deep bitterness towards the British government and towards British rule in Ireland. As a result they were a fertile source of funding for all Irish nationalist movements, parliamentary and military, in the late nineteenth and twentieth centuries." Kinealy, *("Multitext Project in Irish History")*.

Coogan points to Charles Trevelyan as the principal architect of The Great Hunger by following Whig principles of laissez-faire economics: "Famine was at long last solving the English land problem. A surplus and unwanted people were being disposed of." Other historians have had the same view:" Irish all over the world recognize Trevelyan's role. Weighty historians, writing in different eras, in different countries, and with different methodologies, like James Donnelly, Jr. and Cecil Woodham-Smith have stressed the extent to which he [Trevelyan] both initiated famine policies and was given carte blanche to carry them out." Coogan, The *Famine Plot* (101).

Coogan says we should note "the strengthening of the impulse of the Irish public toward helping the Third World, an impulse that has persisted to the present day in the form of donations and aid work." *Famine Plot* (161). John Waters notes that "The Irish experience of Famine provides us with a vital awareness that must guide us towards solidarity with the present victims of colonialism and oppression, for whom in so many tragic instances famine is not yet a metaphor" "Confronting the Ghosts" in Hayden (31).

Sanchez Manning in *The Socialist Appeal* summarizes the courage of the Irish in their history: "The Irish are the great survivors among European nations. They have endured centuries of oppression, persecution, occupation, and attempted extermination: the Vikings, the Anglo-Normans; the attempt by the Tudors to crush them, the attempts by Cromwell to exterminate them; the defeat of their rebellions and the horrendous ordeal of the famine. All these things they have overcome. . . ."

Some families like the Kavanaghs and others survived the Famine and its aftermath.

Finally with the help of Charles Parnell and the Land League, Parliament began to loosen its hold on Ireland: "The Wyndham Act of 1913 allowed most Irish tenants to purchase their holdings from their landlords with British government assistance." (The History Place--Irish Potato Famine). Centuries of English domination came to an end in 1949: "seven hundred years of British rule in Ireland was ended as The Republic of Ireland was finally proclaimed. . . "(The History Place—Irish Potato Famine/After").

THE FUTURE

The figures on hunger in the Third World are staggering: "More than 920 million people in the developing world do not have enough to eat." "Almost two million children in the world display low weight for their age," most in South Asia. Colin Sage, "Food security, food poverty, and food sovereignty" Quoted in *Atlas* (658).

Cormac O'Grada in "The Great Famine and Today's Famines" *Atlas* explains that in the 1990s Irish aid to Third World countries was not very high but has since increased: "What is distinctive about Irish overseas aid is the high share of non-governmental agencies, and the generous and spontaneous response to Third World Disasters"(650}.

Since 1995, the Irish have contributed several million pounds to famine relief in Rwanda, Malawi, and Niger. In 1994 at the opening of the Strokestown Famine Museum in Roscommon, Irish President Robinson spoke of her country's attitude toward food disaster: "The past gave Ireland a moral view-point and an historically informed compassion on some of the events happening now."

Besides the donations, Catholic priests, sisters, brothers and laymen have taught and helped the Third World countries as missionaries, bringing education and food to these benighted nations.

According to Connell Foley, "Ireland is playing a leadership role in international hunger-related programmes. . . ." "Fighting World Hunger in the Twenty-first Century" *Atlas* (669). The Irish Hunger Task Force focuses on owners of small farms, especially women in Africa. It also concentrates on mothers and children's nutrition. Finally, the Task Force ensures that governments give hunger the importance it deserves.

TODAY

*Queen Elizabeth II standing alongside President Mary McAleese at the
Garden of Remembrance in Dublin on the first day of her state visit.
(.bbc.co.uk/news/world-europe)*

In 2012 England's Queen Elizabeth visited Ireland and spoke of their
shared history. What follows is her speech.

"A hUachtarain agus a chairde (President and friends).

Madam President, Prince Philip and I are delighted to be here, and
to experience at first hand Ireland's world-famous hospitality.

Together we have much to celebrate: the ties between our people,
the shared values, and the economic, business and cultural links that
make us so much more than just neighbours, that make us firm friends
and equal partners.

Madam President, speaking here in Dublin Castle it is impossible
to ignore the weight of history, as it was yesterday when you and I laid
wreaths at the Garden of Remembrance.

Indeed, so much of this visit reminds us of the complexity of our history, its many layers and traditions, but also the importance of forbearance and conciliation. Of being able to bow to the past, but not be bound by it.

Of course, the relationship has not always been straightforward; nor has the record over the centuries been entirely benign. It is a sad and regrettable reality that through history our islands have experienced more than their fair share of heartache, turbulence and loss.

These events have touched us all, many of us personally, and are a painful legacy. We can never forget those who have died or been injured, and their families. To all those who have suffered as a consequence of our troubled past I extend my sincere thoughts and deep sympathy. With the benefit of historical hindsight we can all see things which we would wish had been done differently or not at all.

But it is also true that no-one who looked to the future over the past centuries could have imagined the strength of the bonds that are now in place between the governments and the people of our two nations, the spirit of partnership that we now enjoy, and the lasting rapport between us. No-one here this evening could doubt that heartfelt desire of our two nations.

Madam President, you have done a great deal to promote this understanding and reconciliation. You set out to build bridges. And I have seen at first hand your success in bringing together different communities and traditions on this island.

You have also shed new light on the sacrifice of those who served in the First World War. Even as we jointly opened the Messines Peace Park in 1998, it was difficult to look ahead to the time when you and I would be standing together at Islandbridge as we were today.

That transformation is also evident in the establishment of a successful power-sharing executive in Northern Ireland. A knot of history that was painstakingly loosened by the British and Irish Governments together with the strength, vision and determination of the political parties in Northern Ireland.

What were once only hopes for the future have now come to pass; it is almost exactly 13 years since the overwhelming majority of people in Ireland and Northern Ireland voted in favour of the agreement signed on Good Friday 1998, paving the way for Northern Ireland to become the exciting and inspirational place that it is today.

I applaud the work of all those involved in the peace process, and of all those who support and nurture peace, including members of the police, the gardai, and the other emergency services, and those who work in the communities, the churches and charitable bodies like Co-operation Ireland.

Taken together, their work not only serves as a basis for reconciliation between our people and communities, but it gives hope to other peacemakers across the world that through sustained effort, peace can and will prevail.

For the world moves on quickly. The challenges of the past have been replaced by new economic challenges which will demand the same imagination and courage.

The lessons from the peace process are clear; whatever life throws at us, our individual responses will be all the stronger for working together and sharing the load.

There are other stories written daily across these islands which do not find their voice in solemn pages of history books, or newspaper headlines, but which are at the heart of our shared narrative. Many British families have members who live in this country, as many Irish families have close relatives in the United Kingdom.

These families share the two islands; they have visited each other and have come home to each other over the years. They are the ordinary people who yearned for the peace and understanding we now have between our two nations and between the communities within those two nations; a living testament to how much in common we have.

These ties of family, friendship and affection are our most precious resource. They are the lifeblood of the partnership across these islands, a golden thread that runs through all our joint successes so far, and all we will go on to achieve.

They are a reminder that we have much to do together to build a future for all our grandchildren: the kind of future our grandparents could only dream of.

So we celebrate together the widespread spirit of goodwill and deep mutual understanding that has served to make the relationship more harmonious, close as good neighbours should always be." "Queen_Elizabeth_II's_visit_to_the_Republic_of_Ireland" *en.wikipedia The Free Encyclopedia.*

Perhaps these words can set a new tone of friendship between the two countries, one that is long overdue--.since the reign of the first Elizabeth. Both England and Ireland face common challenges—a struggling economy and terrorism. We must acknowledge the past but look to the future.

SELECTED BIBLIOGRAPHY

Atlas of the Great Irish Famine. Eds. Sean Crowley, William J. Smyth, and Mike Murphy. New York: New York University Press, 2012. Print.

Coogan, Tim Pat. *The Famine Plot.* New York: Palgrave and Macmillan, 2012. Print.

_____ "The Lessons of the Famine for Today." *Irish Hunger* Ed. Hayden, 1997. 165-177.

Gallagher, Thomas. *Paddy's Lament.* New York: Harvest Book, 1982. Print.

Gray, Peter. *The Irish Famine.* London: Thames and Hudson, 1995. Print.

Hatton, Helen E. *The Largest Amount of Good.* Kingston: McGill-Queens University Press, 1993. Print.

Irish Hunger. Ed. Hayden, Tom, Boulder, Colorado: Roberts Rinehart Publishers, 1997. Print.

Kelly, Sean. *The Graves Are Walking.* New York: Henry Holt, 2012. Print.

Kerr, Donal A. *A Nation of Beggars.* Oxford: Clarendon Press, 1994 Print.

Kinealy, Christine. *This Great Calamity.* Colorado: Roberts Rinehart, 1995 Print.

Kinealy, Christine and MacAtasney, Gerald. *The Hidden Famine.* London: Pluto Press, 2000. Print.

Laxton, Edward. *The Famine Ships.* New York: Henry Holt, 1996. Print.

Luddy, Maria. *Women and Philanthropy in Nineteenth-Century Ireland* New York: Cambridge University Press, 1995. Print.

Miller, Kerby. *Emigrants and Exiles.* Oxford: Oxford University Press, 1985. Print.

Nicholson, Asenath. *Lights and Shades of Ireland.* (1850). Ed. Maureen Murphy. London: Gilpin. Print.

O'Grada, Cormac. *Black 47 and Beyond.* New Jersey: Princeton University Press, 1999.Print.

O'Keefe, Jack. *Famine Ghost.* Blomington, Indiana: iUniverse. 2011. Print.

Poirtier, Cathal. *Famine Echoes.* Dublin: Gill 1995. Print.

Scally, Robert James. *The End of Hidden Ireland.* New York: Oxford University Press, 1995. Print.

The Great Irish Famine. Ed. Cathal Poirtier. Pennsylvania: Dufour Editions, 1995. Print.

The Irish Famine. Eds. <u>Diarmaid Ferriter</u> and <u>Colm Toibin</u>. London: Profile Books Limited, 2004. Print.

The Meaning of the Famine. Ed. Patrick O'Sullivan. Leicester University Press: London, 1999. Print.

Waters, John. "Confronting the Ghosts." Ed. Hayden, Tom. Colorado: Roberts Rinehart, 1997, 27-31. Print.

Whyte, Robert. *Famine Ship Diary.* Ed. James J. Mangan. Dublin: Mercier Press, 1994. Print.

ELECTRONIC SOURCES

http://boarderancestry.com Web. 19 Dec. 2012

BBC *News* – "In full: Queen's Ireland state banquet speech" - BBC.com Web. 29 May 2012

Boyle, Francis . *The Famine Was Genocide.* http://www.globalresearch.ca/the-great-irish-famine-was-genocide/18156

"Britain's colonial shame: Slave-owners given ... " *The Independent*, Web 28 May, 2013.

dochara.com/the-irish/food-history/food-in-ireland-after-the-famin. Web 12 Mar. 2013

.fashionablecanes.com/Irish_Shillelagh.html Web. 5 Feb. 2012

About Frank Leslie's illustrated newspaper. (New York, N.Y.) 1855 . . . . chroniclingamerica.loc.gov. Web. 6 Feb. 2012

irishholocaust.org/officialbritishintent .Web. 6 Feb. 2012

Irelandsown/net//afroirish Out of Africa, Out of Ireland. James Mullin Web. 22 Feb 2013

http://irelandsown.net/holocaust.html Web. 4 Feb. 2012

http://tee2i.org/topics/ireland Web. 21 Nov.2012

http://www.bbc.co.uk/history/british/victorians/famine html Web. 2 Jan. 2013

http://en.wikipedia.org/wiki/1st_The_Royal_Dragoon Web. 4 Feb. 2013

http://courses.wcupa.edu/jones/his480/reports/civilwar.htm Web.21 Dec. 2012

http://www. irish-genealogy-toolkit.com/coffin-ships.html. Web. 20 May 2013

http://tee2i.org/topics/ireland Web.21 Nov.2012

Kinealy, Christine. *The Great Irish Famine* 1845-1850 nde.state Web. 2 Jan. 2013 http://www.historyplace.com/worldhistory/famine/ruin.htm Web. 3 Jan. 2013

http://www.historyplace.com/worldhistory/faminEbibliography.htm Web. 3 Mar. 2012

Kinealy, Christine. *Multitext Project in Irish History*. Web. 17 Nov. 2012

Manning, Sanchez. *"Britain's colonial shame*: *Slave-owners given. . . ." - The Independent*, May 28, 2013

multitext.ucc.ie/d/Charles_Edward_Trevelyan Web.3 Apr. 2013

Phytophthora infestans - en.wikipedia.org/wiki/Phytophthora_infestans Web.12 Nov. 2012

The Nation, Dublin, 6 November, 1847 Web. Nov. 12 2012

"The History Place—Irish Potato Famine" *historyplace.com/worldhistory/famine/ruin.htm*. Web. 3 Mar. 2013

Randall, David. The *Independent | News |* independent.co.uk Web. 2 Feb. 2013

Schmidt, Mark A. "Patriotism and Paradox: Quaker Military Service in the American Civil War." HIS 480, April 18, 2004 .

*en.wikipedia.org/wiki/Great_Famine_(Ireland)*Web) 12 Dec.2012

http://en.wikipedia.org/wiki/Edward_Turner_Boyd_Twistleton Web. 12 Dec. 2012

http://enwikipedia.org/Charles Cornwallis.1st_Marquess_Cornwallis. Web. 12 Dec. 2012

*http://famineghost.files.wordpress.com/2011/07/famine-ghost-excerpt.pd*Web. 13 Dec.2012.

Socialist Appeal -holocaust-the-Irish-potato-famine Web .2 Feb.2013

"The Society of the Irish Brigade" *home.earthlink.net* Web. 11 Nov. 2012

Stack, Pat. *The Hunger Years*. Issue 189 of SOCIALIST REVIEW, 1995 Web. 21 Feb. 2013

Views of the Famine: Compiled by Steve Taylor adminisstaffvassar.edu Web 1 Jan. 2112

Interview with Cahir O'Doherty. Web. 8 Dec. 2012

www.chacha.com Web .12 Dec. 2012

www.irishholocaust.org/officialbritishintent. Web. 11 Nov. 2012